THE BOY SHERLOCK HOLMES  HIS 5TH CASE

THE DRAGON TURN

SHANE PEACOCK

Tundra Books

Text copyright © 2011 by Shane Peacock

Published in Canada by Tundra Books,
75 Sherbourne Street, Toronto, Ontario M5A 2P9

Published in the United States by Tundra Books of Northern New York,
P.O. Box 1030, Plattsburgh, New York 12901

Library of Congress Control Number: 2011922892

Library and Archives Canada Cataloguing in Publication

Peacock, Shane
The dragon turn / by Shane Peacock.

(The boy Sherlock Holmes ; 5)
ISBN 978-1-77049-231-8

1. Holmes, Sherlock (Fictitious character)–Juvenile fiction.
I. Title. II. Series: Peacock, Shane. Boy Sherlock Holmes ; 5.

PS8581.E234D73 2011   jC813'.54   C2011-901226-X

We acknowledge the financial support of the Government of Canada through
the Book Publishing Industry Development Program (BPIDP) and that of
the Government of Ontario through the Ontario Media Development Corporation's
Ontario Book Initiative. We further acknowledge the support of the Canada Council
for the Arts and the Ontario Arts Council for our publishing program.

ONTARIO ARTS COUNCIL
CONSEIL DES ARTS DE L'ONTARIO

Design: Jennifer Lum

Printed and bound in Canada

ANCIENT FOREST
FRIENDLY

This book is printed on paper that is 100% recycled,
ancient-forest friendly (100% post-consumer recycled).

1 2 3 4 5 6   16 15 14 13 12 11

To the magical Hadley Peacock!

ACKNOWLEDGMENTS

Perhaps the research material that has been most helpful to me during the writing of "The Boy Sherlock Holmes" series has not been a book but a map. *Edward Stanford's Library Map of London and Its Suburbs, 1862*, a virtual aerial photograph of the great city in a time before such things existed, has been my constant companion and invaluable ally. This novel, like the others, finds Sherlock scurrying about London, and my map has always kept him in the right place, even situated him under real trees in their correct locations. Leslie S. Klinger's *The New Annotated Sherlock Holmes*, in three volumes has also been irreplaceable, helping me to see clearly into Sir Arthur Conan Doyle's creation and his stories, to add depth to my understanding of the time period in which my tales are set. Charles Dickens appears several times in this series, perhaps most prominently in this book. Observing brilliant British actor Simon Callow's recreation of him on the stage and screen helped me to accurately recreate him here, as did Peter Ackroyd's masterful biography, *Dickens*. At Tundra Books, I continue to be indebted to the brilliant editorial work of Kathryn Cole, an untiring colleague during every Boy Sherlock installment so far, and hopefully for the next and last, as well. Pamela Osti, Sylvia Chan, Jennifer Lum, and Derek Mah all remain big parts of The Boy Sherlock team. And on the home front, I'd like to thank the kids in the house and the other grown-up, Sophie, who listen to every word of each manuscript and let me know when it is fit to go out into the world.

CONTENTS

PREFACE

The vast waters of the Indian Ocean, with its endless horizons and stifling heat, can be mesmerizing. The humid air above the surface begins to wave like the sea itself, and in that wavering Hades men see things. Visions appear upon the water. And so it was for the adventurer that day. A year in the jungles, a year among savages and beasts, a year away from her, had given him the black fever. As his boat drifted out of the Bay of Bengal, by the Andaman Islands, and south past the Equator, he lay trembling on the deck, his men convinced he would be dead within days. But there were dreams prancing in his imagination, ideas dancing in his mind. He opened his eyes. He looked out across the ocean.

And there it was.

"My life is spent in one long effort to escape from the commonplaces of existence."

      – Sherlock Holmes in *The Red-Headed League*

The moment the dragon appears on the stage of The Egyptian Hall theater in London, Sherlock Holmes knows there is something truly wonderful, truly disturbed, about Alistair Hemsworth. It is the late summer of 1869, and the boy feels as if he is a man. He is dressed in a coal-black, impeccably cleaned and brushed secondhand frock coat, the first of his life; all its predecessors were much older. Sitting beside him with her mouth as wide as his, celebrating her sixteenth birthday, is Irene Doyle. And she is the most beautiful girl, no, the most beautiful *woman*, in all of England. Theirs has been a tempestuous relationship, but lately everything has changed. They have been walking out together, she boldly defying her father's wishes, he (seven months her junior), unrestricted in his movements due to the liberal ways of his mentor, the extraordinary Denmark Street apothecary, Sigerson Bell.

Sherlock had been surprised when she told him that this was her birthday and how old she would be turning. He had assumed that she was younger than he. Girls, he was learning, are full of surprises.

But not even they can make a dragon appear.

There are screams in the crowd. Alistair Hemsworth stands in front of jungle trees, a hand on his hip, his chest thrust out, his other arm raised, his index finger pointing at . . . the writhing beast that has materialized on the stage. It is rising up, it seems, from the depths of the underworld below the theater, a remarkable illusion. Even Sherlock can't figure how he has done it. The dragon hisses, it twists in its cage, three-dimensional and rubbery, a muddy green-gray with golden wings – more than eight feet long from head to tail. Women are staggered by it; they shriek and lean on their gentlemen. But Irene Doyle stands upright. Her face is glowing, lit up with excitement, and as she looks at Sherlock and takes his hand, he glows back.

The dragon's hiss seems to have come from backstage and its wings appear to be flapping mechanically – Sherlock thinks he can see thin black strings attached to the wings against the dark backdrop. And yet, the beast appears to be so real! Instead of fire coming from its mouth, a red tongue, forked at the tip and more than a foot long, darts out in a realistic manner, and its shining eyes glare at the audience, animated more by God, it seems, than any human being, no matter how ingenious. If this isn't a dragon, then it is surely an ancient dinosaur . . . somehow brought to life on The Egyptian Hall stage!

Then a sight even more sensational than the dragon appears *inside* the cage *with* the beast. A woman, wearing a headdress and a purple Egyptian robe that is tied back to reveal a skimpy white muslin costume underneath, rises to her feet on long, bare legs and stands in front of the dragon! She looks terrified. *Hemsworth has put his assistant into the cage with the creature!* Her hands are tied behind her back, her mouth gagged and bound. She cries out, but *help!* is the only word that is recognizable. The screams increase from the audience. Women faint, falling back into their seats. Irene squeezes Sherlock's hand.

Hemsworth turns to the giant lizard and produces a sword out of thin air. "In days of old, the venerable saint slew the dragon at the very moment it approached the princess," he cries, "saving both her . . . and his people!"

The dragon is trying to get at the woman. It is shackled and tethered, but as it strains it seems about to break loose. Will it devour her alive, here on the stage in front of all these people?

"BE GONE!" shouts Hemsworth, shaking his sword at the creature.

Everything – the dragon, the princess, and the cage – vanishes from the stage.

The applause is thunderous.

London has never considered Alistair Hemsworth to be a great magician. No one would rank him among any of the legends now plying their arts in this golden age of magic on the city's stages. Yet, this year, throngs of spectators are coming to see him in never-ending queues.

He was not, like most of the others, born to the profession. In fact, just a few years earlier, he was known, if known at all, as an adventurer. Not a great man like Burton or Speke, the likes of whom braved darkest Africa, made significant discoveries, and brought glory to the empire. He was a different and lower sort – an explorer whose exploits were printed in short notes on the back pages of *The Times of London*, a dealer in human cargo who found freaks in Oriental jungles for English showmen. It was even whispered that he sometimes dealt in the ignominious and illegal trading of slaves . . . of any skin color.

His dream, however, he has been reporting to the newspapers during this season of his great success – has always been to be a famed illusionist. An amateur magician since childhood, he long ago vowed that he would become the theatrical sensation that he is today.

But his show is built on a single moment. Everyone in London knows it.

Sherlock and Irene had sat through his fumbling attempt at levitating a female audience member, his awkward sawing and cutting up of another lady, and the amateurish removal of his own head, an obviously fake, porcelain object, severed from his trunk by his beautiful African assistant, and then nearly dropped on the stage boards as he tried to hold it aloft.

But no one laughed, no one booed. Not a word was spoken. Everyone waited for the dragon. And when it came, it didn't disappoint.

The instant the beast and its "victim" vanish, the lights come up. Hemsworth is gone too. There is a buzz in the crowd, voices filling the grand, Egyptian-themed amphitheater with its rich red curtains and white pillars.

"Come!" says Irene, taking Sherlock by the hand again, something he has gotten used to lately; something, he has to admit, he greatly enjoys.

Bit by bit, over the preceding eighteen months, ever since he was involved in the case of the Spring Heeled Jack, he has been allowing her back into his life. On the night he solved that crime, a stunning chance meeting on the streets with Prime Minister Disraeli had ushered in other changes too. Sherlock had been nearly undone by the frightening events of that evening, but the great man urged him to keep pursuing his dreams. And so, instead of staying out of dangerous criminal cases until he was older, as he had been telling himself he should, or rashly throwing himself into them, as he seemed driven to do, he decided to try a different tack: continue to apply himself and his great gifts, even at this young age, to the cause of justice. (After all, this will be his life's work, so he must train.) But until he becomes a man, he must do so only at arm's length. Thus he began, that day, to help the police whenever he could, but in a new way: by investigating crimes from a distance . . . and then dropping clues to Inspector Lestrade's son (who happily promised to keep his source to himself).

Sherlock and his employer have had a marvelous time with this at the old apothecary shop. Mr. Bell is turning out to be a cunning parlor-room detective indeed, though the boy often thinks that the old man dearly misses helping him collar the criminals in person. Bell is fond of recounting his hand-to-hand combat with the Spring Heeled Jack on the cobblestones of a Bethnel Green rookery.

"My boy! It was a fine bit of Bellitsu, was it not? I believe he must have soiled himself with fear when he saw me approaching, warrior cloth wrapped to my cranium, warrior tights gripping my manly thighs, the muscles in my buttocks tensed like the coils of –"

"We don't need to retell that part, sir."

". . . We don't?"

"No sir, too much information always spoils a good story."

"Yes, well, you may be correct, my young knight. Be that as it may, it was indeed a tight spot we were in that night and I well recall that . . ."

On and on he would go, until Sherlock would get up and leave the room, the old man still holding forth. More often than not, Sigerson Bell would be fast asleep when the boy returned.

Holmes has matured a great deal in many other ways during the past year or so. He is now a pupil-teacher most of the time at Snowfields School, and a student for only a special class or two. These days, he is three or four inches taller than the statuesque Irene. She says she likes that very much. And though she also says that she wishes he were still chasing criminals, she understands that his distance from such endeavors, his more careful style of life, is bringing them back together.

He isn't courting danger anymore, so she is safe with him. She also appreciates that he no longer scoffs at her "improper" ambitions. Irene Doyle is not just singing at home this year. She is taking lessons and has even, once or twice, gotten onto a stage in some of the more respectable music halls in the suburbs and actually sung in public. Neither her father nor her much-pampered stepbrother, Paul, knows of it. She isn't giving up on anything she believes in, not even her new, radical political views. Though, in many ways, she is different from when Sherlock first met her, she has always had a deep sense of conviction about everything she does. She was like that when she visited criminals in jails with her father and helped the poor, and she will be like that forever. She has an unconquerable spirit.

Sherlock can feel that energy as she pulls him along the row of seats toward the aisle at The Egyptian Hall.

"Come, let's meet him!"

"Who?"

"Hemsworth, of course."

"But –"

"How do you think I acquired these tickets? Last night at an audition I met someone who knows him. I did very well – charmed them, I'd say – and the manager gave me a card afterward. He told me that if I showed it to an employee here after the show, Hemsworth would see us. I thought I'd surprise you. A clever man is always of interest, is he not?"

She is right. Such an opportunity isn't to be missed. It would be exciting to speak to the illusionist just moments after he has made his famous dragon appear for a fashionable crowd. *How*, thinks Sherlock, *does he do it?*

The man at the backstage door allows them in the moment Irene displays the card. Sherlock is surprised at the scene inside. He expects to see a hive of all sorts of people backstage – perhaps Hemsworth's exotic female assistant, possibly the musicians leaving the orchestra pit, backstage workers, newspaper reporters, hangers-on or admirers waiting for a chance to speak to the great conjurer. But it is eerily quiet. *Is everyone kept away? Are there that many secrets backstage?* The young couple moves down a dim and empty hallway. It is so narrow that their shoulders almost touch the walls. The doorman slams the entrance behind them, and the noise echoes in the corridor.

"I don't like enclosed spaces," says Irene, gripping Sherlock's arm.

They find "His Highness" Hemsworth's dressing room, the one with the star on the door. There are low voices conversing inside. Holmes knocks. The voices stop and there is silence. "Just a moment!" cries the magician. The low voices resume, halt again, and then the door opens without warning, without the sound of footsteps, almost as if the illusionist has flown across the room. There he stands, his white adventurer's suit glistening as if it were under a jungle sun – sprinkled with something glittery to create the effect – his red hair slicked back, his big mutton chops wet with perspiration, and his mustache and goatee primed with oil. For some reason, perhaps it is the heavy stage make up, his face looks false, like an arranged visage on a wax figure in

Madame Tussaud's Museum. He is tall and barrel-chested, holds himself erect, and gestures to them with the thick, strong hands of an explorer, not the delicate digits of a magician. His blue eyes sparkle as his voice booms.

"My, what a handsome couple! To what do I owe this pleasure?"

Irene explains.

"Ah, yes, Mr. Hollingswood, an excellent man. He must feel you have talent, my dear."

Irene blushes.

"I might be in a position to help you, young lady, if Hollingswood thinks you are to be helped. Perhaps I might have you sing to open my show soon? It would be nice to have some variety. I will consider it." Irene's eyes grow large. "Come and see me again." His smile becomes magnetic.

There is a moment of awkward silence. Sherlock and Irene had expected the artiste to invite them into the room, but he remains standing in the doorway obviously intent on speaking to them here, politely but briefly. Holmes can't see past him, but there is no evidence of the owner of the other low voice that had been heard just moments before. Irene doesn't care about that. She is flushed with excitement.

Then there is another voice, coming from where they entered just moments ago. It sounds familiar.

"I don't care whether he is ready for me or not, I am ready for him. He will come with us, in costume or out!"

Down the hallway march five men at a brisk pace. Three are uniformed Bobbies with their truncheons out and serious looks on their faces. And with them are a father and son, both dressed in brown checked suits with bowler hats, the elder with a full mustache and the younger with one in training.

"Sherlock Holmes?" sputters Inspector Lestrade, coming to a sudden halt. "What, in God's name, are you doing here? You've grown . . . you've . . ."

"Miss?" gasps Lestrade Junior, who hasn't seen Irene for a while, "Miss Doyle . . . why . . . you . . . you look charming this evening." He glances at Sherlock and nods. Irene smiles at him.

"It has been a long time, Master Holmes," continues the Inspector, "thank goodness."

The younger Lestrade looks at the ground with a guilty expression.

"Yes, it has, sir." Holmes grits his teeth.

"I see you have come forward in the world, my boy, a little, that is." He examines Sherlock up and down, looking wary. "Stand aside . . . in fact, vacate the premises. You have no interests here as of this moment. This is police business, something you appear to have learned to stay out of." He extends an arm and index finger back down the hallway toward the entrance.

"Police? What is this about?" asks Hemsworth.

Sherlock and Irene step aside and move back up the hallway. The policemen enter the dressing room and slam the door behind them. The instant they do, Sherlock pulls Irene back to Hemsworth's door. He presses his ear to it.

"Collar him, gentleman!" exclaims Lestrade.

"Collar me! What is the meaning of this?"

"You, sir, are in police custody," barks Lestrade Junior.

"I can see that! But for what crime?"

"For murder!"

Irene stifles a gasp and grips Sherlock's arm.

"Murder? Of whom?"

"Does the name Nottingham ring a bell?" asks young Lestrade.

"You can't be serious."

"We are extremely serious. He was found dead this evening –"

"But I was here, performing!"

"Killed some three or four hours ago in a secret workshop, now identified as yours –"

"Mine! I have no such *secret* place!"

"– where you keep your instruments and hatch your trickery. He was killed in the most gruesome way."

"H-How?"

"I suppose you must ask that question," snaps the Inspector, "We . . . we aren't sure how, but we will find out."

"But then, why are –"

"He did not appear for his show this evening. We found his spectacles, clumps of his hair, his blood . . . bits of his flesh . . . and nothing else . . . in your enclave. We do not know what fiendish or magical thing you did, but we will get to the bottom of this. And we will find his body . . . if there is any more of it left to find."

"But –"

"Take him away."

Sherlock and Irene scramble back to the entrance. They hear the illusionist cry, "But why would I kill Nottingham?"

The young couple flies out the door.

"Mister Hemsworth," replies Lestrade, as he steps into the corridor, "do you take me for a fool? All of London knows why."

THE RIVALS

All of London, indeed, knows why His Highness Hemsworth might want to murder the Wizard of Nottingham. The latter is (or at least, was) the greatest magician that England, perhaps the world, has ever seen. He has levitated people high into the air above his audiences, made an elephant vanish, and turned himself into the very form of one of his spectators. Every illusionist who walks the boards is jealous of him. But Alistair Hemsworth has a greater reason than all the others to want him dead.

Mrs. Hemsworth.

Some two years ago, Nottingham had stolen her away from him, as though he were plucking a rabbit from a hat. The affair had thrilled London and filled the newspapers. Some say the Wizard mesmerized her; others that his handsome looks, his large and powerful frame, his fame, his charming ways and wealth, were all too much for her to resist. The Hemsworths were struggling in those days, and the adventurer, who had always left his wife at home in London while traveling, had just returned from his second-last trip to the Orient, and was making another attempt to begin his theatrical profession in earnest. But there was no dragon in those days, just a fumbling magic act, drawing the few Londoners who wanted to see what tricks an adventurer might have up his sleeve.

No one thought it was a fair fight. Nottingham appeared to sweep her off her feet after their first meeting. His Highness had been a difficult husband to live with – there were rumors of domestic violence – she had her divorce within a year, and a new marriage a few weeks later. There was only one curious thing about it. Mrs. Hemsworth, while not unattractive and said to be "extraordinarily full of life," was a relatively plain woman . . . and the dashing Nottingham, the ladies swore, could have any belle he wanted.

Sherlock tries to avoid eye contact with Irene as they walk briskly along Piccadilly Street toward the Bloomsbury area and the Doyle home. He knows what she is thinking. And she knows that he knows.

"Stop," she finally says, gripping his arm and turning him toward her.

"Yes?"

"You know very well."

"Irene, I can't."

"You can't?" Her lower lip pouts out a little, her brown eyes grow large and look up at him. She is taking acting lessons with her singing instruction, and he can see that they are paying off. "Not even for me?"

"Why would I want to get involved in this?"

"Because you think he is innocent and you believe in justice."

"I have no thoughts on his innocence or guilt, one way or the other."

"But you sized him up. What sort of man is he?"

"I have no idea."

"Sherlock! Tell me what you saw!"

He begins walking again, quickly, leaving her behind. But she hurries to catch up. Busy Leicester Square, filled with sounds and colors and people, appears up the street. Though the hour is getting later, things are still in full swing here. Gaily dressed single women parade about, looking to see which men they attract. Music comes from the theaters and coffee houses, there is a hum in the air, and that jingle of harnesses and clip-clop of hundreds of hooves. Irene comes even with him and puts her arm back through his. "You were saying?"

"Well . . . he is thirty-nine years old, left-handed, a native of Birmingham – north side – exceedingly vain, smokes cigars – West Indian variety –"

"But is he a murderer? When you looked into his eyes, what did you see?"

"I am not in the habit of judging others by looking into their eyes. One doesn't build a murder conviction upon such trifles."

"But you looked into his."

"Uh . . . yes. And I saw nothing. He is a performer. You cannot judge them."

"Is that why you have troubles with me?"

It is only too true.

"You are a *girl*, that's the bigger problem."

She smiles.

"I don't think Alistair Hemsworth is a killer and not just because –"

"No, you think he is someone who can help you . . . who has been taken off to jail."

She swallows, "I deserved that. I appreciate your candor . . . always have."

"You had an opportunity and it suddenly vanished. He is out of circulation."

"For a crime he vehemently denies committing."

"They all do."

"That's not true. You forget how many criminals I have met, how many murderers. I think I know a guilty one when I see one. I have developed a sixth sense. It's . . . a woman's gift."

"I have no such ethereal power. But I will admit that a woman's intuition eludes me."

"Frightens you, one might better say."

"It isn't scientific, not in any way, and therefore, not dependable."

"I know what I heard and saw back there."

"And you know that Nottingham stole his wife."

"I admit that he has motivation, yes."

"Which is an enormous factor in any crime."

"But he seemed to be denying that this 'secret' place where Nottingham was found even belonged to him . . . and they don't have a body. A murder without a body? Answer me honestly: should that be a closed case?"

"I –"

Irene pulls him toward her and guides him out of the flow of pedestrians and up against the wall of a building. She moves closer, gently pressing against him. "This last fact intrigues you."

"Well . . ."

"Look at me as you answer, Sherlock."

He can't do it. She is right about the missing body. It is a most fascinating feature and it indeed intrigues him, deeply so, has from the moment Lestrade mentioned it; *a death without a corpse and no murder weapon.*

"You don't need to solve this. I'm not asking you to do that." She presses even closer. "We could just see if the place is really Hemsworth's, and you could show the police that they haven't proved anything yet, put doubts in their minds . . . get His Highness out of jail for a while, at least?"

"*We* shouldn't be doing anything. And even if I were to look into it, what you are suggesting would involve inspecting the crime scene and I've promised myself not –"

"For me?"

"I –"

"You are correct about my bias concerning this. It is important to tell the truth. You know I believe in that. Yes, I stand to benefit greatly from his being released. Guilty, as charged. But if he is wrongfully incarcerated, then no one benefits, and there is certainly no justice."

"Irene –"

"And this will be a sensational case: the whole country will be intrigued. There's been nothing like this since the Spring Heeled Jack was on the loose."

Oh, that was well put. She is devilishly clever. He feels his resistance crumbling.

"Be honest about your desires, Sherlock," she says, putting her arms around his waist. "You want to do this . . . don't you?"

"I –"

"Beyond everything, you need the adventure . . . because you, sir, are bored."

Ah, another marvelous blow, well struck. She knows me too well.

Boredom is like a monster to Sherlock Holmes, like a troll hiding beneath a bridge, waiting to attack him. It haunts him: he fears it as it approaches. He has been trying to keep the fact that he is bored out of his skull to himself. A boy, even a smart one like him, needs action. Thinking, reading about crimes, speculating, even moving about the city arm in arm with the irresistible Irene Doyle, just isn't enough for him. Several times during the last eighteen months, he has almost chased after pickpockets he's spotted plying their trade in the thick London crowds – *oh, to run them to the ground . . . and apply a little Bellitsu to their craniums! To see Malefactor again!*

The brilliant young gang leader has vanished from the streets, his nasty Trafalgar Square Irregulars scattered. Once or twice recently Sherlock has seen Grimsby, on his own now, still looking dark and evil, not having grown an inch.

But the little villain always averts his gaze, turns away from him, and never looks to be on the job. Crew, the other lieutenant, big, blond and silent, with the ever-present deadness in his eyes of a cold-blooded killer, seems similarly disinterested. Sherlock has seen him standing in doorways down alleyways, on the watch . . . but never doing anything in the least incriminating. *How are they surviving? How do they make a living?* The boy hasn't seen any of the other Irregulars, nor has he spotted the two lieutenants together, not since the moment he flushed Malefactor from his secret residence and ran him into hiding. All that remains of his old rival on the London streets is a sense of his presence. Sherlock feels it when he walks near Lincoln Inn's Field, in the way Grimsby and Crew maintain a look of confidence and ease, as if they are still operating, or being operated by a ghostly hand and mind. In some ways, Sherlock fears Malefactor more than ever. He senses that the tall, sunken-eyed boy with the bulging forehead is still weaving his black magic, and will return . . . soon.

Irene has done her best to entertain him by being with him, by visiting the apothecary shop and conversing, or singing while he plays Bell's violin. She also escorts him (or allows him to escort her) to the theater. Plays haven't tended to intrigue him, unless there is an impossibly difficult crime to be solved – which he usually does halfway through, announcing the villain out loud, as if it were a trifle. It irritates Irene to no end. Low operas are better; violin concertos much better; circuses temporarily sublime; and magic shows supreme. But the very best time he ever had with Irene was the evening she took him to see Charles Dickens.

The legendary novelist was appearing at St. James's Hall and the spectators were queued up outside, like cattle waiting to feed. The big theater held more than two thousand people and every space on the green benches was filled. Sherlock will always recall looking up at the beautiful gold-and-red ribbed ceiling, the overflowing balcony that wrapped around the hall, the stark stage before him with its simple backdrop and writing desk – all awaiting the immortal Dickens. The nation's most famous man was about to display his extraordinary imagination, to become his marvelous characters before their very eyes – *Mr. Scrooge might appear* – to show England and the human race its soul.

The gaslights were simultaneously dimmed in the house and brought up on the stage, and Dickens materialized, lit so starkly that his face, the creases in his pale skin, his very eyes, seemed to be just inches away. The crowd rose and the hall shook with the reception, but Dickens didn't acknowledge them. He set his book down on his desk, placed one leg on a wrung, gripped his collar with his hands and said, in a voice as clear as a bell, "*The Posthumous Papers of the Pickwick Club* . . . the Court Room scene." There was another ovation from the audience. And then he read. And as he read he transported every man, woman and child who watched and listened, to a courtroom in a story . . . that seemed more real than the theater itself. Soon, he had his spectators crying with laughter, amazed at the silliness, the ineptitude of his characters, and thus of all humanity. It made Sherlock think of how we all play roles, how we all want to BE someone, someone shiny, more important than who we really are.

When Dickens was done with that passage, he turned to something that made the audience gasp. "*The Adventures of Oliver Twist*," he intoned. And after a dramatic pause, in which he seemed to eye every audience member, said, "Chapter Forty-seven . . . Fatal Consequences." Everyone knew what that meant. He was going to read what he had once promised he would never read . . . the murder of Nancy, beautiful and honest Nancy . . . at the hands of her lover, the villainous house-breaker, Bill Sikes.

Dickens showed no mercy. He launched into the chapter, bringing the Jew, Fagin, to life, lisping and conniving, revealing to Sikes that Nancy had acted as an informant to good people who would take the boy, Oliver Twist, from his clutches and away from a life of thieving on London streets. A rage grows in the vicious thief. Murder is on his mind . . . a crime of passion.

Dickens, it was said, had not been well of late. His hair was thinning, and he looked slight and pale, as if he might be in pain. There were rumors that some of these performances left him prostrate for hours afterward.

Up on the stage he *became* Fagin, then Sikes out on the street, rushing toward the grimy one-room flat he shared with Nancy, so angry that had his pit bull, Bull's Eye, not kept well ahead of him, he might have strangled it with his bare hands.

Sherlock heard women crying around him. Then Sikes did his terrible deed. He struck Nancy with the butt of his pistol, twice to her face. She staggered, bloodied . . . and he descended on her with his club. Dickens committed the crime with his words, with his voice. And when he was finished, he looked out at his audience, to the people to whom he had told the brutal truth. He stepped from his desk and bowed. The applause began quietly, rising to a crescendo, still gaining volume as he exited.

Sherlock was enraptured. Though he had hoped to hear a chapter from *Bleak House* about Inspector Bucket, the first detective in English fiction, he was not disappointed with *Oliver Twist*. It is his favorite novel, a book about a boy and for boys. Sherlock had cheered louder than anyone else in St. James's Hall that evening. Charles Dickens' fame, his energy, his unmatched imagination, fired the boy with excitement. Holmes wasn't bored, not for one second.

"I want to be alive like that," Irene had said suddenly.

Sherlock had turned to her and smiled, both surprised and charmed. "So do I," he replied, barely above his breath.

And now, as they walk home from witnessing the extraordinary events at The Egyptian Hall, where they had seen a real dragon appear onstage, where Hemsworth the magician was accused of the murder of his famous rival in a sensational case filled with enticing loose ends . . . Irene Doyle is challenging him to be alive again.

Who could resist such temptation?

"My boy!" exclaims Sigerson Bell the instant Sherlock Holmes arrives at their door. The old man hasn't even seen him yet; the lad isn't through the outer room into the back of the shop where they live, eat, experiment, and tangle with each other in brutal fashion during Bell's lessons in the arts of self-defense. "I have been awaiting your arrival for I have been considering having us embark upon an investigation of the workings of the digestive system of the mammal, by thrusting our hands up to the elbows into the –"

Then the apothecary sees his charge and stops. Sherlock appears to be upside down. That is because Bell is hanging from the ceiling again, despite the fact that it is nearing ten o'clock in the evening. It is a practice he suggests to his patients, to facilitate the flow of blood to the brain; he also believes it will help correct the extraordinary curvature of his spine, which is in the shape of a question mark. His long hair descends a couple of feet below his scalp like a little white waterfall, and he is completely naked except for a tiny, tight loincloth. But the sudden halt of his speech hasn't been caused by the mere optical inversion of his apprentice – it is the look on the boy's face.

He pulls his feet out from their harness and does a flip in the air, landing perfectly upright, not an inconsiderable performance for a man his age, which is somewhere between seventy and eight hundred and sixty-nine. Thankfully, he fetches a gold-colored smoking jacket and covers himself up.

"What has happened?"

It is an irritating talent: the old man's ability to read Sherlock's face as if it were a screaming headline in *The News of the World*. The boy thinks of himself as being so much more inscrutable than that. But he has learned to live with Bell's great powers of observation and deduction, and also to keep very few secrets from him.

"It was the most extraordinary thing." Sherlock seats himself on a stool at the laboratory table.

"I can see that. Were you not escorting Miss Doyle this evening? Is she trifling with your heart again? Sit down and I shall tender you some advice. I am a man of some experience in the mysterious ways of the fairer sex."

"It is not that, sir. Miss Doyle was most cordial and we had a lovely evening until . . ."

"Until what?" Bell seizes another stool and pulls it up close to Sherlock, seating himself in a flash, his face inches from the boy's, looking deeply into his eyes, irises snapping back and forth. His breath, fishy and full of the aroma of his favorite food – the foreign garlic onion – is enough to knock out a prizefighter. Sherlock pulls his stool back a few inches.

"We went to see Hemsworth."

"Ah! The dragon man! Is it real?"

"It appeared to be."

"I believe it! I believe there are dragons . . . somewhere! Mankind does not invent such stories out of thin air. If there are not dragons, there must be beasts much like them . . . perhaps the dinosaurs still roam on some far-off, undiscovered island!"

"It wasn't that, sir. It was what happened afterward."

"Afterward?"

Sherlock tells him. The old man listens, fascinated. When the boy is done, Bell rubs his chin. "Two celebrated men, a celebrated wife between them, and now . . . a sensational murder. A crime of passion! Irene Doyle has asked you to intervene."

Sherlock, of course, hasn't told him any such thing. This is irritating too . . . how Bell can take almost anything Holmes says and immediately deduce all sorts of other facts. Though the boy knows that he too, is often guilty of the very same maneuver, it still makes him want to scream.

"Yes, she has!"

"And shall you?"

"Uh . . ."

"Ah-ha! I knew it! You are back in harness!"

"I didn't say that."

"Nonsense! Where are we to start?"

"*We?*"

"I mean . . . you."

"The crime scene, of course."

"But you don't know where it is."

"I have the means to find out."

Though the younger Lestrade is not blessed with either Sigerson Bell's or Sherlock Holmes's talent for deduction and observation, he has no trouble picking out the boy far down the street in Whitehall, near Scotland Yard, early the following morning; that, despite the flow of horses and hansom cabs moving along the cobblestones, and the pedestrians strolling on the footpaths. Holmes, of course, doesn't dare stand on the south side near the police buildings. He is at the gates of the Admiralty across the thoroughfare, doing his best to look respectable and purposeful in his secondhand suit. He has a morning paper clutched under his arm, having plucked it from a dustbin. The Hemsworth arrest is splattered across the front page, though there is little of real news in it for Sherlock, other than the curious fact that Mrs. Nottingham has not yet been located by the police. Aware of the spectacular nature of this case, Scotland Yard is being tight-lipped about everything, including the location of the crime scene.

It is a Saturday morning, but Sigerson Bell, unable to resist his young charge's interest in the sensational Hemsworth case, in fact, anxious to hear more of it himself, has given the boy several hours off from his chores at the laboratory. Cleaning bottles and flasks and polishing the three statues of Hermes can wait until noon.

Lestrade knows there is no sense avoiding Holmes.

Most days, he would be pleased to see the brilliant young half-Jew. The clues the lad has provided him over the past year or so have been most helpful not only to his career, but to his father's opinion of him, and that is important, indeed. But the unfortunate coincidence of Holmes's presence at The Egyptian Hall last night, in company with Miss Irene Doyle no less, has not been sitting well with young Lestrade all night. Now almost nineteen years old and a fully paid police employee, he is officially embarked on his career and lives for it. He never takes a Saturday off; and sometimes even comes to headquarters on Sundays, without saying a word to his father. Holmes, he knows, would be just as thoroughly pursuing a detective's career of his own sort . . . if he weren't younger and, most curiously, holding himself back.

The scrawny police detective in the loose, grown-up clothes always notices the lust for fighting evil in Sherlock's eyes, and his effort to control it. That effort, as young Lestrade feared from a distance, does not appear to be present today when he sees him up close. He owes Sherlock Holmes, and that isn't a good thing this late August morning.

"Master Holmes."

"Master Lestrade."

"I must apologize . . . I am in a most frightful hurry this forenoon."

"Well, that is a coincidence, so am I."

"You are?"

"I am. I must be at the scene of the Nottingham murder and back to my school at Snowfields within the hour. I am teaching summer classes."

"You . . . must?"

"I must."

"Well, you see . . . there is only one problem with that."

"I am all ears."

"And nose, too."

Sherlock doesn't smile.

"Master Holmes, as I'm sure you are aware," he glances down at the newspaper under Sherlock's arm, "the location remains a secret . . . you know I can't –"

"Nonsense."

"I hadn't finished."

"No need to. You shall tell me what I need to know. You forget, I am in a position to blackmail you."

"By telling my father that it has been you who has been supplying the clues for our cases lately?"

"Precisely."

"I would deny it. And he would believe me."

"I am in possession of many details of those crimes. Details only one with a –"

"All right!" snaps Lestrade.

"Where is it?"

"If you so much as move one –"

"Where *is* it?"

Lestrade looks back at Scotland Yard and then lowers his voice.

"The Cremorne Gardens."

"Excuse me?"

It seems like a strange choice for a secret anything. The Cremorne is London's loudest pleasure gardens, filled nightly with couples in pursuit of fun, gentlemen in pursuit of ladies (or so they call themselves), and ladies in pursuit of them (and their money). Balloon ascensions, high-wire walks, educated dogs and monkeys, minstrels, freak shows, fireworks, and dancing and more dancing take place within its fancy wrought-iron gates – twelve acres of undiluted amusement.

"Hemsworth has a secret studio in the Cremorne Gardens?"

"At The World's End Hotel, below stairs. It seems he inhabits it at night."

"Thank you."

"Sherlock, you cannot go there. We have it sealed. Constable Spears won't let you through."

"When does he leave?"

Lestrade hesitates. "He ensures that the doors are locked when he goes home each night. I am sorry."

"Never mind that. When does he leave?"

"Uh . . . there will be no one there after one o'clock in the morning, though an officer shall return at six. So, you can't –"

Sherlock begins to walk away, but pauses and turns back.

"Who found the body?"

"There was no body, Master Genius. We told you that."

"I stand corrected. Who found the Wizard's blood, the little bits of him, and his spectacles?"

"The hotel keeper."

"He just happened to wander downstairs that day?"

"I shan't tell you more."

"Lestrade, you know I shall discover this anyway. Withholding evidence will only slow things down."

The young detective sighs. "There is a boy, a street urchin who lives in the area and sleeps in the Cremorne. He sees everything. He used to watch for Hemsworth at night, who would slink through the Gardens in a long black coat and safari hat, looking around, sneaking his way toward the hotel. It amused the boy, so he'd watch for him every time. The child has an over-active imagination. He said he knew the man was a magician or a wizard of some sort because he saw him do strange things: he'd always enter through a secret outside door at the back, which he'd open simply by speaking to it, and summon some sort of creature inside . . . that sort of fantastic stuff."

"So, it was the boy. He got inside? He found the blood?"

"He noticed that Hemsworth was accompanied by another man a few nights ago, but only Hemsworth came out. Then the magician didn't appear again for a day or two. The boy simply mentioned this to the hotel keeper. So, the keeper went downstairs. There was no answer at the inner door that led to the studio from the hotel . . . he went inside."

"And the boy knows for sure that the other man never appeared again, didn't leave through an unknown door? He positively identified this long-black-coated man as Hemsworth?"

"Holmes, what wishful fantasy are you driving at? The second man wore clothing identified as Nottingham's. The cloaked man wore a black safari hat, known to be favored by

Hemsworth. It was Hemsworth's place. We know that. It was clear once we were inside. He took Nottingham in there and left without him, without his body, that is."

"Did the *keeper* say it was Hem –"

"Don't start making assumptions, like you are wont to do, trying to fit your theories to the crime. Criminal investigations are about facts, and facts alone. We are in possession of other evidence . . . which I shan't share with you." He pauses. "Sherlock, please, don't go there. Leave this alone."

Holmes departs Denmark Street about half past midnight that night, bearing one of Bell's small blades – with a particularly sharp tip – to help pick the lock, or to protect himself, though he also has his horsewhip concealed up his sleeve. It has rained most of the day and the air is thick and humid. The yellow fog has returned. He will have a long walk tonight, but he knows the streets and how to keep clear of the criminals, the straggling drunks, and prostitutes. He moves stealthily through London, head on a swivel, first down the frightening, narrow streets near his neighborhood to a nearly-deserted Leicester Square, then along Piccadilly Street past The Egyptian Hall, spotting Buckingham Palace in the distance to his left. Then he is into upper-class Belgravia, turning off Knightsbridge Road before he reaches the unlikely area where Malefactor had his home. He checks for a pursuer more than once here and feels for his knife. Then he swings south, by leafy parks and racket courts, until he reaches King's Road, and goes west into Chelsea. Soon he can smell the river and see the Battersea Bridge and the lights of the saw mills and chemical works on the other side of the Thames. Moments later, he approaches the Cremorne Gardens.

Its gaslights are dimmed and all is quiet, which is eerie for such a place. It is as if death has come to the Cremorne – everything has been stilled.

The Gardens is surrounded by a wrought-iron fence and its main entrance is on King's Road, a beautiful black gate with a gleaming star on top. Sherlock climbs the fence near the padlocked entrance and goes in. For a place that exists for entertainment, some of it the most crass in the empire, the Cremorne is beautiful. Elm trees hang over lush, emerald-green lawns and there are flowers everywhere. He heads into the misty jungle, under the few remaining lights, passes the big circus building, the Marionette Theatre, the American Bowling Saloon, and the central dancing platform. Then he creeps carefully through a more open area, along a tree-lined lane in the shape of a figure of eight, keeping his head down until he nears the south end of the park.

The hotel is looming there: The World's End. It's a fitting name. It looks spooky enough during the day, just two storeys high, but long and black, with turrets at each end, as if it were home to a colony of vampires. At night, with all its lights out, it seems even gloomier. He approaches. He hears crows cawing from its heights and rats scratching and squealing around its base.

His heart, much to his annoyance, begins to pound in

his chest. At the back, the building is lined with a wall of trees. They tower over him now – weeping willows and copper beeches, looking like monsters ready to defend the hotel from a rear attack. Suddenly, a wind comes up and moans through the branches.

Sherlock sees a shape moving toward him in the darkness.

Sherlock grips his knife. But as the figure moves closer, he can see that it isn't very big. In fact, when the moon gives him a clear view, Holmes is sure it is a child. But what a strange child: it is difficult to tell, at first, if this person is a boy or a girl. It is not only short, not much more than four feet tall, but so slender as to be skeletal. The eyes are sunken, the brow and cheekbones stick out, and the complexion, marked with filth, is bluish-white, like bones underneath the skin. The hair, growing long and unkempt under a hat made of nothing but a brim, is the color of dirt. But those eyes are large and blue, and full of expression, the lips thick and active.

"Might a lad be of assistance, guvna?"

His voice isn't as high-pitched as expected, though it quavers a little. He doesn't seem to be able to stand still as he talks.

Older than he looks, perhaps twelve or thirteen, frightened but trying to appear not to be, grew up somewhere in the center of London, perhaps Seven Dials, homeless, orphaned. This is the boy Lestrade spoke of!

The lad's shoes are barely shoes. All ten toes glow white in the moonlight. His once royal-blue trousers are full of holes, and three or four sizes too big, held up by green suspenders, which is the only clothing covering his upper body. Holmes can count every one of the little lad's ribs on his milk-white torso.

"Yes, actually, you might be helpful," smiles Sherlock, trying to put the other at ease.

"At your servicement. I am employed 'ere. Security, for the 'otel, you know."

"Your name, sir?"

"Scuttle."

"As in . . . Scuttle . . . butt?"

"No sir, just Scuttle, no family name presently attached."

"It is a pleasure to meet you."

"Kind of you to say, guvna, but Scuttle shan't be swayed by gleams and pleasantries. I must 'ave your name and then repulse you away from The World's End 'otel. I keeps them all away, I do, even the famous ones. No one is allowed 'ere late at night, courtesy of the unparallel patrolling of yours truly. And I makes no expections, I don't. I've seen 'em all."

"Them all?"

"Famous celebrantites comes by the Cremorne all the times, you know. Scuttle knows 'em all, speaks with 'em I do. I knows the queen."

"The queen?"

"Spoke to 'er, Scuttle did, and she gabbed back. And I said 'ello to Mr. Dickens . . . twice."

"*Charles* Dickens?"

"The wery one, Scuttle leered at the famous explorer Richard Francis Burton too. 'As spear wounds in 'is face, 'e does. Conversated with 'im. I've looked at the famous famed Florence Nightingale, and . . . the Spring 'eeled Jack . . . of course."

"You don't say?"

"Scuttle does say so, sir. Do you doubt me?"

"Not for a moment."

"I needs your name and then you must excavate the premises."

"I won't be telling you my name. I am about to enter the hotel."

"But . . . Scuttle wouldn't allow the famous Miss Menken 'erself to enter, that woman who rode 'alf naked on the 'orse in the London opera named *The Wild 'orse of the Mazeppa*, which meant so much to all of English civilization. No, I wouldn't allow . . ."

"You know there was murder here yesterday."

"I . . ." the boy's face somehow turns whiter than it was. "'Ow do you knows that, guvna?"

"Master Scuttle, I am a confidante of the police."

The boy swallows. "Scottish Yard?"

"The very one."

"Well, you must be, sir, because Mr. Starr, who runs the 'otel, 'e told me 'bout the murder just hours past, said no one else knew, told me on the QT, 'e did."

"You are to inform no one that you saw me, not even other detectives. I am with a very special department." Sherlock lowers his voice. "This is *extremely* secret."

"Yes, sir."

"I am in disguise. I am actually thirty-five years old."

The boy looks at Sherlock in awe.

"Scottish Yard 'as solved many famous crimes, sir, they is renowned, sir. Scuttle's lips is sealed, glued shut so as to never move again. I shall looks away and pertend as to 'ave not viewed you in the least."

The boy turns his back and marches off, without once looking over his shoulder. In the dim light, Sherlock sees an open-ended dustbin, turned over in the trees nearby, the boy's likely home for the night.

"I have a question for you, sir," says Holmes, "before you retire."

The small boy stops in his tracks. He still doesn't look around. "Scuttle is at your commandment."

"Where is the secret door?"

There is a long pause. "I am loathe to say, sir, but in the servicement of Scottish Yard, I shall unveil it. It's the door the magician used."

"Mr. Hemsworth?"

"Yes, 'is 'ighness 'emsworth, 'e of the great dragon trick that means so much to all of London, and to Scuttle, as well. I gabbed with 'im too, 'e who has broken our hearts by murdering the Wizard of Nottingham. 'e who –"

"Where's the door?"

"Just walk straight up to the middle of the towering trees, sir. You will spy two copper beeches. Go in betwixt them. It is below stairs, big and wooden, big enough to shove a hippopottingmess through, covered with moss."

"Thank you."

"Be on your best guarding, sir, it is a place of magic and mysteryism. Scuttle believes this crime was the result of a war of wizards and somehow Nottingham, who is the best one, you know, lost . . . and ended up completely dead!"

Sherlock finds the door. It sits at the bottom of a long set of stone stairs, well below ground. He gingerly descends on the wet slabs. At first, he thinks the door has no handle or latch, no way to penetrate from the outside; but searching in the moss, his fingers find a keyhole. Out comes his knife, and within moments, feeling around in the hole as he's seen Malefactor teach his minions to do, he springs the inside latch.

Though the boy is trying to remain calm, he is almost beside himself with excitement. He has forgotten how thrilling it is to be this close to murder, injustice, and danger. He feels a sort of euphoria waft over him, the kind of sensation he imagines the apothecary's patients must experience when they take their medications: their mixtures of cocaine or laudanum. They always become so happy.

The door, of course, creaks as it opens. Sherlock stands at the threshold, listening. For a moment, he thinks he can hear someone, or something (for it sounds a good size), breathing. Either he is imagining it, or the thing stops, for soon there is silence. All he can hear now is the crows outside.

He steps inside and closes the door. It is pitch black. He's had the presence of mind to bring a candle, and a Lucifer from Sigerson Bell's match jar, both of which he now draws from a pocket. He strikes the Lucifer and the moldy air is filled momentarily with the smell of phosphorus and lit by an intense flame, which then lessens. He lights the candle and looks about.

It is just a single chamber, but enormous; a cavernous workshop with stone walls, perfect for a magician who needs room to practice tricks, especially the large, showstoppers that Hemsworth has always tried to enact. *No one could hear you down here either.* It's open in the center, as if cleared for space. The walls are lined with thick wooden tables, almost bare, except for a few items, unidentifiable at first, in the dim light. Sherlock moves toward them with his candle and, as he does, his peripheral vision catches a glimpse of something on the floor. He stops dead in his tracks and almost cries out. At his feet are streaks of red, then a congealed puddle, a pair of spectacles, and what almost looks like small, dried pieces of flesh. The boy gulps. *The remains of Nottingham, left untouched because the police investigation is ongoing.* He examines where everything is positioned. It almost looks to him like this was staged. He goes around the blood and over to the tables. On the one directly in front of him, closest to the murder scene, sitting between a dark tropical plant and a pot of maturing mushrooms, he finds a top hat. He looks at the band inside the lid and sees the initials *A.H.* imprinted there.

That is indeed a telling piece of evidence. Hemsworth's hat is so close to the blood. They have him, almost literally, red-handed. But why would he leave his topper here, for the police to find? Was he interrupted during the act and had to flee? Was he too overwrought, not thinking straight, during his crime of passion? Sherlock glances at the little flecks of flesh. *How, in God's name, did he do this?*

He picks up the hat and examines it. *Rather large.* When he was younger, he had briefly believed in the art of phrenology – the examination of skull sizes and peculiarities in order to size up the intelligence of individuals. A bump in one area might mean talent in the arts, another elsewhere, perhaps an aptitude for alchemy. He has long since rejected this pseudo-science, mostly at the insistence of Sigerson Bell, who has taught him that it is the brain, not the skull, one must examine. And the size of the brain is not all that is important either: intelligence is a deep and abiding mystery. Sherlock has noticed how some people use phrenology to say terrible things about other races – find a few Africans with small heads, for example, and you have proof of their inferiority. But the boy has never lost his interest in skull size – observe *everything*, his scientist father taught him – and this is helpful when pondering which hats might fit particular heads. He frowns at this large lid now, remembering Hemsworth's modest skull. He sets it down, wishing he had the accused in front of him.

Then he examines the room more closely, and what he discovers only adds to his questions . . . and suspicions.

One of the many shows Irene Doyle has taken him to see over the past year and a half was a performance of the unmatched skills of the Wizard of Nottingham upon The Egyptian Hall stage. They saw him guillotine a woman and then bring her back to life, vanish in front of their eyes, and read the minds of reputable men in the audience. Nottingham did everything with a showmanship and deftness that was, Sherlock imagined, unparalleled in the world of show business. But even at such events, Holmes was ever the detective-in-training. He made it is his business to memorize everything about Nottingham – the color of his hair, the way it was combed, the size of his skull (a lovely big one), the turn of his nose, the tint of his spectacles, and the clothes he wore.

Now, as he examines Alistair Hemsworth's "secret studio," he finds a few pieces of clothing that match Nottingham's stage costumes lying on the tables, a couple of props identical to those used in his acts sitting on the shelves above, and standing in a corner . . . a guillotine. Hemsworth had not used such an instrument during his act.

But Sherlock's intrigue is immediately arrested. There is only one window in this cavern, and it is tiny, just inches tall, with an iron bar crossing it, right up near the ceiling. One might stand on one's tiptoes on a stool and look out, but outsiders could never see in through its narrow, thick glass.

Holmes spots a light flash in the window, swaying back and forth, like the effect a lantern would have if it were being carried. The light is moving around the side of the hotel . . . toward the back.

Is someone coming in the direction of the secret door?

Sherlock scrambles away, almost slipping on the blood, and makes for the entrance. As he does, he thinks he hears something again, something moving, not in the room, but somewhere near. There's no time to pause. He is at the door and has it open in seconds. He closes it with a bang so the latch will lock, and takes three wet steps at a time up the stairs.

"Who goes there!" shouts someone. It isn't Scuttle. It's a man.

By the time he gets to the top of the stairs and feels his feet on the moist grass, he thinks he is safe. But an arm reaches out from the trees and seizes him.

"Got you! Your name, sir?"

Sherlock looks into the face that is glaring at him. *A businessman of some sort, working class, hotel industry, awakened from his sleep, forty-five years old.* The man is a good two or three inches taller than him and the boy can tell by his grip that he is as strong as an ox. He wears big Wellington boots and a black bowler hat . . . and a red dressing gown covers the rest of him.

"My name?"

The man's face is adorned with a dark brown mustache and goatee. It and his hair are disheveled. He has indeed been roused from his bed.

"Leopold Leotard."

Both the man and Sherlock turn in the direction of the little figure who has just spoken.

"Master Scuttle, do you know him?"

"Yes, sir, I does. And a right fine gentleman 'e is. I will voucher for him."

"I pay you to watch my place, you young scamp, and I won't look kindly on you allowing anyone near here, especially now amidst all this kerfuffle."

"Yes, my keeper, sir, I am on alertment at all times. I knows this lad, this Leopold . . ."

"Leotard. You said 'Leotard,' didn't you? But . . . wasn't he that flying-trapeze star, who got the ladies all aflutter a few years back?"

"Uh . . . that was that gentleman's name too, sir, yes it was. And a wery important man in our civilization, sir. The sensation of London at the time, and of the world now. This 'ere gentleman just happens to have the same name, though 'e might 'ave 'ad relations with 'im."

They both turn to Sherlock.

"No, gentleman, I am no relation to Monsieur Leotard, though I am flattered that we bear the same family name."

"What were you doing here, Mr. . . . Leotard?"

"'e was just strollin', sir. Said 'e 'ad trouble sleeping. We 'ad a chat, sir, just as I gab with the most famous folks who –"

"Yes, Scuttle, I know, you converse with famous people and become acquainted."

"Cross my 'eart, I does."

"Thank you, Scuttle, now be on your way."

"Right, sir. A blissful good evening to both of you nubile gentlemen."

Scuttle, who notices that the hotel keeper is examining Sherlock, winks at his new friend before disappearing into the mist toward his rude bed.

"My name is Harrison Starr, Master Leotard, or whatever your name is, and if I find you anywhere near here at night again, I shall call the constabulary and have you put in irons. There are things occurring here that you know nothing of, boy, and you had best avoid. Do you understand me?"

"Yes, sir, I do, sir."

The man shoves him in the direction of the Cremorne's main gate. Sherlock turns to face him.

"Sir, I must say that whatever you may think of me, I am impressed with you."

The man sighs. "How so?"

"You pay that poor boy."

"Hardly pay."

"What do you mean?"

"I give him scraps from the hotel tables. He is an idiot with an intelligence barely exceeding that of my bull mastiff . . ."

"Might I ask another –"

". . . which, I shall set upon you if I *ever* see you again . . . even in broad daylight upon the street!"

IRENE TO THE RESCUE

Sherlock is awakened the next morning by a startling but enjoyable vision – the face of Irene Doyle. Her big brown eyes are within inches of his. For a moment, he simply smiles, assuming it is a dream. But when he reaches out to take her face in his hands, the soft skin and cascading blonde tresses feel real. He leaps to his feet, smacking his head against the top of his wardrobe. Irene doesn't budge, in fact, her smile grows.

"Good morning, Mr. Holmes, any news?"

Sherlock is wrapping his oversized nightshirt around his torso, looking down to make sure there are no holes in this worn-out gift from Sigerson Bell.

"Where . . . where is my master?"

"Out of doors early this morning. Said he had an emergency appointment. He noted that you often oversleep, especially on Sundays, and told me to go ahead and wake you."

Sherlock frowns. He can imagine the old man laughing all the way down Denmark Street.

The boy seizes his black trousers and white shirt from a nearby stool, takes them into the wardrobe and slams the doors behind him. He struggles as he tries to get them on in the tight space. He had once allowed a frightened girl named Beatrice Leckie – who used to be his friend – into the lab in the middle of the night, and Irene had actually picked the lock and stolen in another time. On each occasion, he was required to greet them in his nightshirt! *Why are these females constantly barging into my bedroom?*

"You haven't answered me, Sherlock."

"What did you ask, Miss Doyle?"

"Any news?"

"Of what?"

"Sherlock, get out of that stupid wardrobe immediately and speak to me. Do you think the sight of a boy's bare chest will shock me?"

Two years ago, yes. Now, unfortunately, no, not at all.

She swings open the doors. Neither his trousers nor his shirt are done up. He puts his back to her.

"Turn around, Irene."

"Oh, Sherlock."

"Turn around!"

She obeys, though she peeks at him, noting that Sherlock, though still very slim, has put some meat on his bones. Irene is wearing a gorgeous purple dress, which flows to the floor and down her arms to the wrists, where the silk is trimmed with bands of black velvet. She is obviously *not* going to church this Sabbath. She has been a little ahead of fashions for the last few years, and this dress sticks out at the back, at her rear end, in fact, the effect created by something called a bustle. It is the "coming thing" for young ladies in the know.

The boy finally finishes and allows her to turn around. Her appearance, in full view, is stunning, even more so than he is used to.

"I . . . I . . ."

She looks down at herself. The dress is cut a little low on the chest. For a moment, she actually blushes all the way from her face, along her neck, to her visible collarbones, and the old Irene is momentarily standing in front of Sherlock. But she gathers herself.

"Oh, this thing," she says, glancing at it. "Father is livid about me wearing it, especially on a Sunday morning. I understand, but it is really more of a costume than anything else: I am to sing this afternoon for Mr. George Leybourne, no less. He wants to hear me, and I can't miss the chance. I will be back at church next week. But never mind that, what is your news?"

"I went there."

"You did?"

Sherlock isn't giving her his full attention. He is hungry, a constant state for him these days. The old man usually has something edible in the icebox. The boy creaks open the door and looks inside. There it is. It isn't exactly breakfast fare, but he doesn't care.

"Blood pudding?" he asks Irene. She gives him the look of someone who has just been asked to eat a tasty serving of vomit.

"Some tea, then?"

She nods her head, and he takes the oozing, bright red sausages from the ice box and begins to make a repast. But she keeps him on the subject.

"And?"

"And what?"

"You are the most irritating –"

"It isn't Hemsworth's workshop."

Her eyes grow large. "Honestly?"

"I think it is Nottingham's. I found a guillotine, clothes that look similar to what he wore the night we saw him at The Egyptian Hall, a few identical stage things . . . and Hemsworth's hat."

"Oh, no."

"Right near the blood and spectacles."

"*Right* beside them? But why would he leave it there? Isn't that a little suspicious?"

"I thought so too, Miss Doyle." Sherlock lights a bunsen lamp and places three blood sausages in a pan on a tripod over it. He lights a second lamp and boils the tea. "And it's too big for him."

"What?"

"The hat: it has his initials on it, but it looks awfully large for him."

"That *is* interesting."

"But not something I can prove. I would have to place it on his head."

"So, why can't –"

"What chance do you think I have of doing that? And I might be . . . wrong."

"But if the studio is Nottingham's, then there are important flaws in the Yard's case."

"Maybe."

"Why were they so sure that it belonged to Hemsworth?"

"Young Lestrade says they have evidence."

"Of what sort?"

"Found at the scene of the crime."

"They must mean the hat. But that isn't enough, especially if it doesn't fit Hemsworth. If you can prove to them that everything else in the studio belongs to Nottingham, then you can create some doubt . . . and then get them to try the hat on –"

"Remember, it has Hemsworth's initials on it. It is a long shot, at best. And young Lestrade won't listen to me anyway, not about something like this. His father made the arrest and won't go back on it without irrefutable evidence. His son won't try to budge him, you can count on that. He is awfully ambitious these days and won't rock the boat on this one, believe me. Even though it's a Sunday, I'll wager he is at Scotland Yard right now, working on the case, filing papers without even the Inspector's knowledge."

She smiles. "The young detective will listen to *me* though. Did you not see his reaction when we met at the theater?"

Yes, he was smitten, Irene, as is every male who meets you. You didn't used to be so aware of that.

"We shall use *all* the weapons we have at our disposal, Sherlock . . . to fight for justice. We'll have Hemsworth out of jail in no time!"

"I beg your pardon?"

"I will be back within the hour."

"Where are you going?"

"To Scotland Yard."

She is out the door before he can protest. But within moments, there is a knock. He grins, assuming she has reconsidered, realizing the futility of her attempt; that even her charms will do no good at the Metropolitan London Police Headquarters. He opens the door without looking through the peephole.

"Irene, I —"

"Irene? Who's she?"

It's Beatrice Leckie.

"Beatrice?"

"Sherlock," she says shyly, barely able to look at him. Even in her black scullery maid's uniform with its flowery white and grey trim, there is something about her that keeps him from closing the door. Her porcelain-white skin, curly black hair and matching eyes as dark as the night, and most of all, the kindness in her face, all conspire to draw the boy's attention. She, too, has grown up a great deal over the past eighteen months, and is a striking young woman now. But Sherlock remembers the way she deceived him during the Spring Heeled Jack troubles; how she actually helped the fiend, how she made a fool of him. *It was embarrassing.* She appears so simple on the surface, but Miss Leckie is much more than she seems. He has barely spoken to her since. *She deserves that,* he tells himself. *I can't believe how fondly I once thought of her.* Beatrice keeps looking up, her eyes on his. He casts his own away. She has been calling at the shop for several months now, and her calls have increased the last few weeks, but he has never even opened the door to her . . . until now.

"What do you want?"

"Who is Irene? Is she the Doyle –"

"That is none of your business."

"I was called in to do extra work by my employer on this side of the river, for a few hours this morning. I was passing by 'ere on my way 'ome. May I come in?"

"I don't think that is a good idea."

"Sherlock, I did what I did because I believe in justice, like you. It 'urt no one, though it may 'ave 'elped some. There are those in need who –"

"What do you want?"

"It's your father."

A moment later, they are sitting at the table in the back room.

"Is that black pudding?" she asks.

"Uh, yes . . . would you like some?"

"I would! There are some who turn their noses up at it, you know. But I recall when we all used to eat it at 'ome. Remember? You and me, we often shared –"

"Have you seen Father?"

"That's why I came."

"How is he?"

"'e is still working . . . but I don't think 'e should be."

Holmes blanches. "Why?"

"'e isn't well, Sherlock. 'e looks awfully thin and 'is beard and 'air are going very gray. It's 'appened over a matter of months."

"Gray?" He thinks of his strong father, his hair and beard as black as a crow, brilliant and full of integrity, forced from teaching science after his mixed marriage to Rose Sherrinford, now working at the Crystal Palace, caring for the doves of peace. The boy thinks of his own role in his mother's death . . . of his strained relationship with his father after that. Sherlock knows he should be seeing him, trying to make things right. It has just been too hard to face. Occasional letters back and forth have been short and few. The boy tries not to think of the past. *It is gone. What is the use?*

"I wonder," says Beatrice, "if something is terribly wrong."

Sherlock stiffens. *Whatever is wrong, it cannot be fatal. Wilberforce Holmes cannot die. He should live forever. He should live to be a hundred years old in that flat the Crystal Palace officials provided for him after his wife was murdered. No . . . he shouldn't. He should grow younger, have his beautiful Rose return to life, live his dreams, exist in a world where no one hates a Jew who marries an English lady because he loves her.*

Something else runs through the boy's mind. *Sherlock Holmes . . . orphan.* He tells himself that Beatrice must be exaggerating, that his father is fine.

"Tea?"

"But —"

"I shall go to see him. I am sure he is well, likely just overworked. Tea?"

"Uh . . . yes."

He hands her the flask intended for Irene, not remembering that Miss Doyle said she would be back soon. He fills it to the brim. Once he pours his own, there is none left.

Beatrice tries to smile and takes his hand. Though her hand is not quite as soft as Irene's, he is surprised at how remarkably warm her skin feels.

"I could go with you to see 'im."

"That won't be necessary."

"But you might need –"

"I don't need anything."

There is an awkward silence.

"You are right. You don't need anything. And you certainly don't need me in your life. I betrayed your trust. I should go."

She gets to her feet.

Holmes is feeling vulnerable. He hates that. He is frightened about losing his father. Beatrice Leckie has known him since he was a small child. She worked for the Spring Heeled Jack for admirable reasons, he knows that: she was being brave, and honest, and concerned for the poor, the well-being of others, as she always has been. And she likes him: not for what heights he may someday reach, but for who he was as a boy and who he is now. She would like him if she knew nothing of his recent accomplishments, if he were still simply a poor half-breed, bullied at his school.

"Don't go," he says, reaching out and putting his hand on her shoulder.

She sits immediately, surprised.

"Well . . . shall we eat black pudding?" she asks.

"Yes, we shall."

Half an hour later, in the midst of their laughter over an old story from home, the outside door rattles open, and closes.

Sherlock leaps to his feet. "Irene!"

She comes through the front room and into the laboratory, veritably shining with energy and beauty. Glowing in her purple silk dress and bustle, she already looks like the star of the stage she hopes to one day be. On her arm is Lestrade Jr.

"I have brought you a visitor!" But before she can launch into her story, she stops in surprise, seeing the plain-dressed girl who has replaced her at the lab table, having drained the tea that was intended for her.

"Who is this?"

"Uh . . ." says Sherlock.

"Have we met?"

"I believe we 'ave, once, very briefly. I am Beatrice Leckie, an old friend of Sherlock's."

"Friend?"

"Yes, a friend. You must be Miss Doyle. 'e speaks 'ighly of you."

"He does?" Irene pauses, then steps toward the girl and takes her hand. "Any friend of his is a friend of mine. Yes, I believe we have met."

"I was just leaving." Beatrice rises.

"She was," says Sherlock.

"Nonsense, do not leave on my account. I have brought Master Lestrade here for a most interesting discussion. Would you like to hear, Miss Leckie?"

Beatrice sits down again.

At first, Lestrade feels as though he is in heaven. Not much more than half of an hour ago, the beautiful Miss Irene, she of the irreproachable Doyle family, burst into his new office in Scotland Yard, like a breath of fresh air and began flattering him many times over for his recent detective work. Then, she asked if he would take her arm and escort her home, saying she wanted the air and felt much safer with him. Now, he is also in the presence of the beguiling Miss Beatrice Leckie, whom he hasn't seen for more than a year, but whom he remembers from the Spring Heeled Jack affair. He recalls that he was angry with her role in helping the fiend, but right now, as she smiles back at him, he finds it difficult to summon even the least bit of resentment. He sits and removes his hat. Irene Doyle . . . Beatrice Leckie: he hardly knows which way to look. But he figures it out . . . when he finally notices that Sherlock Holmes is at the back of the room, and hears Irene mention the Hemsworth case. He glares at the other boy. Miss Doyle hadn't said anything about the murder during their walk. The young detective knows that she lives on Montague Street and wondered why they had turned down Denmark Street and entered this apothecary shop. He had imagined it was just a stop on the way to Bloomsbury and she had needed to purchase something. He is well aware that Sherlock is employed by an apothecary, but with his mind elsewhere, it wasn't at the front of his thoughts that Holmes might be apprenticed at this particular establishment. Suddenly, he is conscious of being expertly seduced. His face turns red.

"Is this why I was brought here?" he says, pointing at Sherlock, looking like he wants to get up and go.

"Stay seated, sir," says Irene, "Master Holmes has some news for you."

"I am not in need of news."

"In fact, you are," says Sherlock.

"I shall decide if –"

"It isn't Hemsworth's workshop."

". . . That's preposterous."

"And the hat is too big for him," adds Irene.

"Nonsense. It has his initials on it!"

Sherlock details what he found in the basement of The World's End Hotel. He even mentions Scuttle and his interaction with the hotel keeper.

"First of all," retorts Lestrade, "I told you *not* to go there. Secondly, just because you eyeballed a magician's skull size from the fiftieth row of a theater, and then found a few items at the crime scene relating to the deceased –"

"The deceased?" interjects Beatrice. "I read that you didn't have a body . . . only his spectacles and some blood."

Sherlock smiles and Irene notices.

"That is all we need, Miss Leckie," replies Lestrade quickly. "They were enemies, Nottingham stole his wife, it is Hemsworth's studio – we have a young witness who saw him enter many times – and it *is* his hat! Nottingham is missing – exploded to death or some such thing. Hemsworth has always envied the Wizard – he likely had the guillotine there to copy him, clothes like his for similar reasons. We have no doubt who our man is."

"But Sherlock's evidence seems worth investigating," says Irene, taking her eyes from Beatrice and turning to Lestrade.

"Evidence? Speculation, I'd say! My father will laugh at it."

Holmes gets to his feet and turns his back on the other boy. Irene isn't pleased either. "Well, *I* think it's enough to make you re-examine your evidence, to consider allowing Mr. Hemsworth temporary freedom . . . until you are certain."

"Oh you do, do you? Scotland Yard does not!" Lestrade has had enough of Irene Doyle.

"Have you found Mrs. Nottingham yet?" asks Beatrice.

Lestrade is getting it from all sides. He glares at Miss Leckie and says nothing.

"That means no," says Sherlock.

"That means you do not have the right to inquire, *any* of you!"

"But if she is missing, shouldn't she be a suspect too?" asks Irene.

Lestrade is steaming. He gets to his feet.

"Might I simply ask you this?" inquires Holmes through his teeth, still looking away. "Who actually *owns* the studio? Hemsworth may live there, or perhaps Nottingham. We can look into that. But who *owns* it? Is it one of them? Surely, you have searched the records."

"Yes, surely we have! And if you must know; if this will stop your pestering: it does *not* belong to Nottingham. His name is *not* on the ownership. Satisfied?"

"And Hemsworth's is?"

"Not exactly."

"Not exactly?" asks Beatrice.

"Miss Leckie, it is *not* appropriate for you –"

"Whose is? Whose name is on record as the owner?" asks Irene.

"We believe it was being let to Hemsworth."

"Let to him? From whom?" asks Irene.

Lestrade pauses again. "This is the last thing I will say and then you will all leave this to the proper authorities. The owner is someone who would have no motivation to murder Nottingham. He is a businessman, a Jew, named Riyah. We . . . cannot locate him at present."

And with that, he leaves the shop.

Holmes knows he shouldn't return to The World's End Hotel that night. And he also knows why he's doing it.

"You must go back, Sherlock," said Irene not long after young Lestrade left the shop that morning. She had walked over and seated herself close to him. Until then, the two girls and the boy had been silent. "You need to fetch the hat. If you can, I am sure we could find a way to get the Lestrades to try it on His Highness's head. My father might help."

"It might not matter who helps. If Hemsworth is brought before the magistrates, our esteemed inspector might convince them that modeling the hat isn't necessary, despite any pleas that we or even the solicitors for the defense might make. The police will point out that it was found in the accused's workshop, that his initials are on it, and do so in the midst of presenting *all* that motivation. Any protestations would be waved off."

"Then we have to get the hat onto his head *before* he is in court. Perhaps I could arrange a visit, sneak it in, and slip it to Hemsworth in his cell. Then we could force the

Lestrades to take a look. But whatever we do, we need that hat, and we need it now."

"I suppose I –"

"Steal evidence from a crime scene?" asks Beatrice. "What would they do to you if you were found with it? You can't afford to take this chance, Sherlock, not with everything going so well at school, with your 'opes for university. Perhaps there is another way."

"And what way would that be?" asks Irene.

"Well . . . I could go. That 'otel is frequented by working-class folks, lots of people in the service. I wouldn't stick out. People talk after they've 'ad a few drinks. I could learn more about this Jewish owner, about –"

"And you aren't without charms, my dear, and can use them to get the keeper to talk? We need the hat." She turns to the door. "I must be going. I must get to my audition."

"But Sherlock," pleads Beatrice, "you can't –"

"You aren't going there, Beatrice," says Holmes firmly. "And you won't be involved in any way either, Irene. *I* will take care of this."

The boy is again bearing the knife and horsewhip when he leaves the shop. Bell is fast asleep, or so it seems. It is another misty night. As he drops over the gates at the Cremorne, this time making absolutely certain that no one is nearby, he wonders why he let Irene convince him to do this. Maybe he should have listened to Beatrice. *She is the one who has my best interests at heart. Or is that true? How can I be certain, after what she did? Irene believes in justice and that's why she is encouraging me. She's more like me; she knows who I want to be, instead of who I was. And she is the dazzler of the two, no question.*

Sherlock becomes lost in his thoughts as he walks through the dark Cremorne jungle surrounded by the now-quiet, show-business venues. He smiles as he thinks of his remarkable female friend.

Why not live a little? Why not escort Miss Doyle about London? I couldn't have dreamed of such a thing just a few years ago. She has a good heart too. She knows you have to take chances and stand up for what you believe in. She has made so much more of herself than she might have been, more than most girls dare. Irene believes in being truly alive. That's what I want too.

He has allowed himself to think so absent-mindedly about the girls in his life (always an error for a detective) that he doesn't see Scuttle creep up behind him.

"Ass-sign with Scottish Yard again, sir?"

Sherlock nearly jumps from the Gardens into the River Thames. When he calms down, he thanks the stars that the little boy is whispering tonight.

"Yes, Master Scuttle, though we must be quieter this time."

"I shall be as silent as the bedbugs infesticating my mattress."

"You have a mattress?"

"Of a sort. I gets fresh horse dung each night and wraps it in straw from the Cremorne stables, I does."

That would explain the smell.

"Scuttle, would you be a good lad and stand guard tonight? One knock means someone is nearing, two means I must come immediately. Do it lightly."

The small lad scratches his head. "Can you repeats that?"

Sherlock does.

"I thinks I 'ave it. But can I 'ave a badge?"

"No, Scuttle. We are –"

"Ah, yes, under the covers, of course. Excellence!"

"Ssshh."

Sherlock's hands are shaking so badly that it takes him a while to open the latch, but at last he is inside the workshop, closing the door gently behind him so it doesn't creak. He takes a single, tentative step and listens carefully, not moving a muscle, not even lighting his candle. Just as on the previous night, he hears a sound. He stands stock still, holding his breath. *Pay attention to it this time. Where, exactly, is it coming from?* He doesn't advance another step for a long while and slowly calms his breathing to the point where no one could detect it, unless they were inches from his face. Soon, he hears the sound again. *Faint footsteps?* He keeps still. Then there's a different noise: a cough, a human cough in the distance, but somehow, not outside. *Somewhere to my left.* He treads silently toward it, each step carefully taken. The sound comes again. It is apparent that it isn't originating from inside the room or from the hotel above. *How is that possible?* It's like magic . . . or a ghost – a sound with no origin or cause. This is a single, large room. There are no doors other than the secret back entrance, and another directly in front of him, which must lead up a staircase to The World's End. *I can't go up there.* The walls are made of stone: they are basement structures, thick and certainly forming the foundation of the building. The cough comes a third time. It is as if there is someone . . . or something . . . *inside* the wall!

Sherlock takes a chance and lights his candle, gambling that the sound of the igniting Lucifer won't be heard through the wall. He examines the shelves in front of him. They are filled with books. He scans them, noting the titles on the spines. The boy isn't impressed. There are no Dickens novels, no Eliot, no Collins, no Virgil, no Greek myths or Shakespeare. Instead, they are about magic, or thin biographies and gossip about current stars of the stage, the circus, and sporting endeavors. But one title stops him. *The Existence of Dragons.* It is the thickest of all the volumes. He plucks it out, sets the candle down on the floor and turns to the first page. It is blank. He flips through the book. *That's strange. Why is every page blank?* He stands up and replaces the book. The cough comes again, right in front of him . . . most definitely on the other side of the wall. He pulls the dragon book out again, holds the candle up and looks at the surface behind the shelf. There is an indentation there, a large, round indentation, and there is something not quite right about the wall surrounding it. He touches it. *It doesn't feel like stone.* It is made of some sort of imitation material. He presses on the indentation. Nothing happens. He braces himself against the bookcase and presses with all his might. He hears something, a sort of rumbling . . . a few strides to his left. He steps that way and sees a foot-and-a-half of space between the shelves.

The wall behind it is moving!

Sherlock darts into the space and through the opening. It slams shut behind him. He turns and searches along the imitation stone, but it's sealed up again. Immediately, heavy breathing drifts through the dank air, and then the cough. It's directly behind him. Clutching the blade inside his coat, he swings around and flashes the light toward it.

There!

A figure in a dark coat is blowing out a small candle on a table, rising from a chair and beginning to run away. It isn't the keeper. Sherlock pursues it.

"You! . . . Scotland Yard!"

The boy is quickly aware that he is in a surprisingly large room, even bigger than the main part of the basement he has just come from. Here, unlike in the other space, the shelves are crammed full with tools of the magic trade – top hats, wands, shiny clothes, wigs, cages, cartons of cards, and caskets for body-severing tricks. They are piled high along all the walls. Sherlock recognizes many of the things that Nottingham used in his act.

The figure keeps fleeing. It seems to know where it is going. Holding up his candle, Sherlock can see a huge opening in the wall in the direction they are running, and what appear to be stairs descending from there. *Descending? To where? Another, deeper chamber?*

The man stops suddenly. He hesitates. Then he turns to face Sherlock.

"So sorry," he says in a German accent, "I should not be rushing off, but you startled me. Vhat do you vant? Vhy are you here?" He coughs again. It sounds a little forced. "Excuse me, I always cough in enclosed spaces."

Before the boy stands a man in a long black great-coat, so long it almost reaches the ground. He wears a black felt hat, pulled down almost to his brow, below which two dark eyes look out from a face full of whiskers. His black hair falls almost to his shoulders. Other than those eyes and a big, unusually hooked nose, his face is mostly hair.

About sixty years old, hiding something.

"Who are you?" gulps Sherlock.

"It only seems right zat you should answer ze question first, sir," says the man, sweating and gasping a little for breath. "After all, *you* are in *my* territory."

"My name is Holmes . . . and I am in the employ of Scotland Yard."

"Are you, now?"

"Yes . . . I am."

"Und vhy should I tell you who I am?"

"Because there was murder done here and anyone on the premises is a suspect."

"Including yourself?"

"I said I was in the employ —"

"Yes, of Scotland Yard. You vill have to prove zat, should you vant to get out of here alive."

"I . . . I have a guard outside the door. If I do not reappear soon, there will be trouble for you."

"But I am difficult to find, sir. You know zat yourself. Ze vall is sealed. I could simply leave your body in here."

"I . . . I am armed." Sherlock lets the knife slip down his sleeve and into sight.

"So am I," says the man, and he pulls a revolver out of his greatcoat and points it at Sherlock's head. "I always carry zis late at night."

There is silence for a moment. Holmes begins to sweat. The knife handle feels slippery in his hand. He thinks he hears something, a sort of rustling, coming from the inner chamber down the stairs.

"I tease you, my boy," says the man, putting the gun away. "But you should not be here. Come. I shall escort you back to ze main room. I know ze hocus-pocus that will move ze vall again. It is another button on ze inside!"

"Your name, sir," says Sherlock, still pointing the blade at the man. "You have not given me your name."

"I am Riyah, Oscar Riyah."

When they return to the main room, Riyah begins to explain. In fact, he seems to be in a talkative mood.

"I own ze property, ze hotel, und all of ze below stairs."

"Why have you not come forward, spoken to Scotland Yard?"

"I am a Jew, you know. My father vas one, at least. I am one of zose evil money-grubbing Jews . . . und I prefer to not be associated vis any murders, you vill understand. I am sure ze police can do zeir job vizout speaking vis me."

Sherlock doesn't tell him about his own Jewish blood.

"Do they know about the inner chamber?"

"Vhy are you asking me? I thought you vere vith zem. Or don't you remember?" He winks at the boy.

"I . . ."

"No need to explain. You are an acquaintance of ze boy, Scuttle, I imagine, but a little more curious, and brighter, shall ve say?"

"Yes, sir."

"I don't believe zey know about ze inner chamber, no. And ve shan't inform them, shall ve?"

Why is he telling me all of this? Why doesn't he just throw me out?

"What about the other chamber?"

"Other?"

"The lower one. I saw an opening and a staircase descending."

The man's face darkens. "Did you, now? Zat's too bad."

"I . . . I won't say a word."

"I have never been down zere."

"But you own it."

"Vhen I purchased zis building, zere vere stories about a dungeon beneath it, used by Villiam ze Conqueror in ze 11th century. Men vere tortured in it, put on racks and stretched until zeir limbs snapped. I . . . have no interest in going down zere. Why would I?"

"But I heard a sound down –"

"I have heard zese sounds too. But I zink it is just vater trickling, or deep gasses gurgling beneath ze earth."

"But –"

"I would not be surprised," continues the Jew, "if Nottingham went zere zough. Perhaps he keeps his doves and rabbits zere."

"Nottingham?"

"Yes, I let ze premises to him."

"I thought so!"

"You are pleased?"

"I have a friend on the Force, not much older than I. His father is Inspector Lestrade."

"Ah!"

"That's . . . that's the reason I'm here. You might say that I am an *unofficial* police employee, and I discovered how to get in. It has been my belief all along that the studio belonged to Nottingham."

"Vell, you are correct."

"You must tell the police! They think it's Hemsworth's."

"As I said, I prefer to keep out of such zings. A Jew's reputation is sullied enough in England by his mere existence."

"Sir . . . I am part Jewish."

"You are?"

"I understand our situation, believe me, but you cannot let an innocent man die."

"I am sorry, but I haf told you my reason, and it shall stand. It is my impression zat ze identity of ze tenant vill not swing ze case one vay or ze ozer, my boy. I vould come forth to ze police if it might. What does it matter if Hemsworth was renting it or Nottingham? Ze Vizard is dead and His Highness had good reason to do it. Let ze law take its course. Nottingham vas my tenant and I vant zis dealt vith immediately. Zey have zeir man!"

Sherlock's head drops. There is nothing else he can do. He can't even take the hat. *How could I explain that? I can't steal evidence in front of the owner.* Since Riyah won't come forward, Sherlock doesn't even have proof that the workshop belongs to Nottingham. "I have to get out of here."

"So, you are a Jew too, you say?"

"Part."

"And zat vas difficult for you, yes?"

"Very."

"For me too, my son. I even changed my name. Before I came to zis country, I vas known as Abraham Hebrewitz."

Sherlock's head snaps up, but not at Mr. Riyah. He is looking over his shoulder and across the room . . . in the direction of the hat.

"Sir, have you misplaced your hat?"

The man's eyes brighten. "Vhy yes! I haven't been able to find it for several days. How do you know zis? Are you some sort of magician yourself?"

Sherlock walks over to the hat and shines his candle on it. It is almost hidden between the tropical plants and pot of mushrooms. Riyah turns around and sees what he is doing.

"Zat's it!" cries the Jew. He tucks it under his arm and does a jig. "My hat! My hat! My gloriously expensive old hat!"

"Sir, we must be quiet!"

But it is too late. There is a rumbling above, then a thudding coming down the inner stairs from the hotel.

"I have to go! *Now!*" cries Sherlock.

"Not so fast!" Riyah reaches out and seizes the boy by the arm. Suddenly, the sixty-year-old man seems much younger and much stronger than before. There is a glint in his eye as he holds Sherlock and twists his arm with great skill, the sort of martial arts hold that Sigerson Bell might apply. The boy feels as though his arm will be pulled from its socket if he attempts to move. Riyah is hiding the hat behind his back.

The inner door to the hotel slams open.

"Got you!" cries the keeper, glaring at Sherlock. Then he notices who is holding him. "Mr. Riyah!" The name is spoken with the respect due to one's economic better, and nothing more. "I haven't seen you for a while, sir. It's just as well that it's you who caught this scamp because we have been trying to find you. Now we have you both. This boy has been here before; last night, in fact. I will send Scuttle to get the police."

"No need," says Riyah in a surprisingly soft voice as he releases Sherlock from his grip. "It vas I who brought zis boy here. I noticed him outside, loitering about, und asked him in. I thought he might like to see ze crime scene. Zere is no harm. You vill recall your own boyhood interest in sensation, no doubt?"

"Why, yes, sir, I suppose. But you must remove him, now . . . if you will. And make your own way to police head-quarters, sir. They are anxious to speak with you."

"I prefer to stay out of zis, Mr. Starr. You vill tell zem zat you have not seen me. Hmm?"

"But –"

Riyah reaches into a pocket of his greatcoat, pulls out a few coins and passes them to the keeper.

"Yes . . . sir. But . . . even you cannot come here again, not for the rest of the week. The police are forbidding anyone to be here. I went to their offices earlier today to tell them that I found this boy near the back door last night. They were not pleased. They are worried that word may spread about this location. So, beginning tomorrow, they will have it guarded around the clock until Hemsworth is sentenced, which should be shortly."

The Jew's face darkens. "I see. Zat vill be all, Mr. Starr. We shall find our own vay out through ze back."

Riyah sends Sherlock on ahead, to shoo Scuttle away, not wanting to be seen by the ever-vigilant and conscientious younger lad. Holmes asks him if they can meet by the Garden's gate – there is something he must tell him.

A few minutes later, he sees Riyah lumbering toward him, his hat under his arm. The boy almost runs to him.

"Sir, circumstances have changed."

"Changed? What do you mean?"

"The hat . . . you either need to take it back and leave it where you forgot it a few days ago . . . and let Mr. Hemsworth go to his death. Or come with me to Scotland Yard, this instant, and tell them that this topper belongs to you."

"I don't understand."

"The police think it is Hemsworth's hat."

"Zhey do?"

"And, as you know, they think it is his studio."

"But ze hat obviously belongs to –" Then Riyah nods. "Ah, yes, our initials, *A.H.* . . . zey are identical."

"You said you didn't come forward because it didn't matter. It matters now, sir, believe me."

Three hours later Mr. Riyah and Sherlock are sitting on a wooden bench in the foyer of Scotland Yard off Whitehall Street when Lestrade senior and junior come blustering into the office looking angry and lacking in the last few hours of their Monday morning beauty sleep. They are accompanied by a uniformed policeman.

"Sherlock Holmes!" spurts the older detective the instant he sees the boy. "You didn't mention he would be here, Constable Monroe. I'll have your job!"

"Knew you wouldn't come if I mentioned 'im, sir. But 'e's the one who brought in Mr. Riyah. That's the 'otel owner, sir, right there with the boy."

"Riyah! He glares at the older man. Why in the name of the queen didn't you come forward before! We have been looking high and low for you! Monroe says you have valuable information, sir. It had better be good! Out with it! A man's life is at stake."

"I let ze studio below ze Vorld's End Hotel to Mr. Nottingham, Inspector."

"You do? Well, that is of some interest. What is that accent, sir?"

"German."

"Hmmm."

"Und zis," Riyah produces the hat, "is mine."

Lestrade's eyes nearly bulge out of his head.

"It is?"

"It is."

"Preposterous! Your name is Riyah! The initials on the inside are —"

"I changed my name some time ago . . . after I bought ze hat."

"From what?"

"Does it matter, sir? I can prove it."

"I believe Mr. Hemsworth is innocent," says Sherlock, stepping forward.

"Well . . . I . . . I *don't* believe it!" shouts Lestrade.

"Father, you must –"

"Close your gob, sir. I will handle this. The day may come when you can tell me what to do, but it has not arrived yet. Outside of your mother, I am the boss . . . of me!"

"Sir?" says Sherlock, "Shall you let Mr. Hemsworth go?"

"Let him go? . . . NO!"

"No?"

"This man may prove that he has changed his name and his true initials may indeed be *A.H.*, but . . . can he still prove that this is his hat!"

"But ze hat, sir, it is, I bought it many years –"

"Many years ago? Do you have a bill of sale?"

"No sir, zat would be imposs –"

"Aha! Hemsworth shall be tried for the murder of his rival. It does not matter if he did it in Nottingham's workshop or his own. He did it. He had ample motivation, more motivation than I have ever seen in a crime during all my years on the Force. It makes perfect sense. And this may very well be his hat, anyway. Perhaps you and the accused have the same kind? This is a common topper, my good friend."

"No, sir, I am sure –"

"And why would *your* hat be there anyway? Answer me that!"

"Surely, sir," interjects his son, "Mr. Riyah cannot be a suspect. He owns the premises. He must be there often. He simply forgot his hat. He has no reason to murder –"

"What did I say about interruptions, young man?"

His son closes his mouth.

Riyah looks frightened. "Perhaps you are right, sir. I shall just take ze hat and be on my vay. I am sorry to have inconvenienced you. I shall give you vhatever information you –"

"Shall we try it on?" asks Sherlock, stepping right up to the senior detective. The latter is a bit disconcerted, not only by the close proximity of the half Jewish boy from the streets who has bested him several times over the last few years, but also by the fact that he has grown so tall that their eyes now nearly meet. Sherlock Holmes's peepers are just a few inches from his.

"I beg your pardon?"

"I challenge you, sir, in front of all these people."

There is indeed an audience. The shift at Scotland Yard is about to change and a number of officers have been arriving during this confrontation. Intrigued by the contents of the argument and the raised voices, they have gathered in the foyer. A good-sized crowd of Lestrade's charges now surround the actors in the drama.

"I challenge you to try this hat on Hemsworth's head."

Lestrade looks around. All eyes are on him. He turns to his son and whispers, "It's just a regular topper, isn't it, my boy? Should fit, shouldn't it?" But the boy is reluctant to respond. He doesn't have a sure answer.

Silence fills the room.

"All right," says Lestrade eventually, "all right. Bring the prisoner forth and we shall put his hat on his head. Remember, Holmes, if it fits, then it is his, correct?"

"Correct."

The quick response unnerves the senior detective a little more.

Hemsworth is retrieved, looking sleepy. His face is not arranged as expertly as it is when he is upon the stage. He eyes Riyah and Sherlock and everyone around him.

"This boy and this gentleman," begins the Inspector, "think that this hat, found at the crime scene, in fact right next to poor Nottingham's blood and spectacles, is not yours. I want you to try it on. This will decide your fate, sir. Do you choose to attempt it?"

Hemsworth visibly swallows. He looks at the hat. "It *isn't* mine," he says.

"Prove it."

"Can . . ."

"And should you choose to model this headgear and are wrong, no lawyer in the empire, one would guess, will be able to save you."

"But –"

"Make your decision!"

Hemsworth takes the hat in his hand and holds on to it for the longest time. Silence descends on the room again. His hand is shaking. Slowly, ever so slowly, he raises the hat toward his head.

"Be quick about it!" barks Lestrade.

Hemsworth holds it above his red hair. He moves it around carefully, looking up at the brim. From where Sherlock stands, it looks like a perfect fit. *What will Lestrade do to me if I am wrong? Does it make sense to judge a man's head size from the seats of a theater? The magician's cranium looks bigger up close.*

Hemsworth lets the topper fall gently onto his head, tipping it slightly forward. It sits there . . . a perfect fit.

Lestrade lets out a roar. He turns to Sherlock Holmes, a deep smile on his face, a smile he has wanted to unleash upon the boy for a full eighteen months, ever since the lad solved the case of the Spring Heeled Jack. The Inspector is about to say something when Hemsworth suddenly speaks up. Everyone turns back to him. He waits until they are all watching.

"Oh, I beg your pardon," he says, "there is a saying in the world of magic that one should fail at least once whilst performing any effect, before one does it correctly. That, you see, primes the audience, builds up the tension, and moves them to applause at just the right moment." With that, he tips the big hat back and it falls clean over his small skull and down to his shoulders. Everything from the base of his neck up is now . . . a hat. "I believe," he crows from inside the topper, "this lid is a little large!"

The gathered policemen burst into applause. All, that is, except two.

BIG MISTAKE

There is no show that night at The Egyptian Hall, but both Sherlock Holmes and Irene Doyle are in attendance the following evening when Alistair Hemsworth makes his triumphant return to the London stage. The magician has made sure that they have front row seats. Inspector Lestrade, who was also favored with a pair of ducats, is nowhere to be seen.

No one, not the boy, the Inspector's son, or any of the other policemen, thought they had ever seen Lestrade's face redder than it was at the instant Hemsworth magically let the hat fall over his skull to his shoulders. It looked like the respected policeman's head might explode, an act of spontaneous combustion about to happen right in front of them. Sherlock had barely been able to control himself: he had wanted to laugh out loud.

"Release the prisoner!" Lestrade had cried. "And get this boy out of my sight!"

Hemsworth, who appears from the shadows and into the spotlight this evening to a gigantic ovation, is in his glory. If he had thought he was the toast of London before, now he knows he is its idol. His Highness performs the dragon feat this evening as never before – the beast looks more lifelike than ever, the Egyptian-robed princess's horror seems *very* real. All is magnificently rendered and the crowd is captivated. And afterward, Sherlock and Irene are, once more, invited backstage.

"Do you think he will ask me tonight?"

"Pardon me?"

"Sherlock, you really are a man-in-training, aren't you? Do men not hear what women say because they block out higher-pitched voices?"

"I don't know –"

"I am wondering if he is going to ask me to sing for him, to see if I might appear in his act. Remember? What an opportunity this would be!"

"Oh, yes, of course, Irene. I hope he asks you."

"You are thinking about something else, aren't you? Sherlock Holmes: the boy with his head in the clouds!"

His mind is indeed on something else. But his thoughts aren't happy ones. He is worried. It began when he rose this morning. He doesn't know why, but getting Hemsworth out of jail just seemed too easy to him. Even Sigerson Bell had looked surprised at the news. *Am I really getting so good at this? The Lestrades were convinced of Hemsworth's guilt. What if he really did it? What if I helped free a murderer? Did I do it just for Irene?* He thinks of his mother and what was done to her by a criminal. *Justice is what matters, not pleasing someone whose attentions I seek. Girls can be dangerous.* He tries to set aside this guilty feeling; he should be enjoying himself. Irene says he isn't very good at that.

The doubts don't leave him as he walks toward the star's dressing room. *Hemsworth has never once appeared to be the least bit upset about Nottingham's death.* Sherlock is uneasy about the hat-modeling scene at Scotland Yard too, concerned that the magician was acting throughout, and knew all along that the topper wouldn't fit. It all seemed so theatrically done. *Was it just his flair for the dramatic?* There is something about His Highness that the boy doesn't like. He recalls hearing those whispers in the dressing room the first night they met. *What was going on? Was Hemsworth just being a performer then too? Everything he does is for an audience, it seems, even when he walks down a street.* Sherlock has heard it said that the magician is a little crazy. *Maybe he was whispering to himself?*

"Welcome! Welcome!" shouts the triumphant performer, his wax-like face well put together once more. "Miss Irene Doyle, future singing star of the stage . . . and Master Sherlock Holmes, young detective extraordinaire."

There is no one else in the dressing room; this will be a private audience with the great man, while others line up outside in the hall. Or at least . . . it appears to be just the three of them. From the moment Sherlock enters the room, he has a sense that they are not alone. There is a curtain drawn across one end of the room. The boy thinks he sees it flutter once or twice. Irene doesn't appear to notice, but then again, her mind is on other things.

They have a long chat, filled mostly with conversation about the funny scene at Scotland Yard. Sherlock doesn't say much and wonders if Hemsworth notices. But the magician seems to be very excited tonight, eyes sparkling and cheeks red, not given to noticing any subtleties of behavior. His interest in them only sputters after a good ten minutes of holding forth.

"I am afraid I must see others as well. It is too bad. I would prefer to speak with you two young people all night!" He stands. "I shall see you out."

"Uh . . ." Irene stops herself.

"Yes, Miss Doyle? Was there something you wanted?"

Sherlock can't believe this cad doesn't remember what he promised her.

"Sir . . ." she begins, "it's just that . . . you . . . never mind."

"Mister Hemsworth," says the boy. "Do you not recall suggesting that Miss Doyle might audition for you for the purpose of participating in your magic act?"

His Highness looks startled. "Why, yes, of course! I am so very, very sorry. Of course! I shall send my card around to you soon, Miss Doyle. Montague Street, is it?"

He knows where she lives, thinks Sherlock.

Irene nods, her face glowing.

The magician then brings their visit to a close. Irene leaves the dressing room first, looking back, smiling. Sherlock follows, trying to seem friendly, but not able to pull off much of an acting job. Just as he is almost through the door, he thinks he hears a faint cough. He stops.

"What was that?"

"What?" says Hemsworth.

"That sound."

"I didn't hear anything. Thank you for visiting. I am in your debt, sir." Hemsworth grins at him, but the expression looks forced this time. He puts his hand on Sherlock's back and applies gentle pressure, ushering him from the room. "I should speak to a few more folks." He motions to the next couple waiting in the hallway. They enter to the magician's cheery greeting and the door closes.

That cough. Was Hemsworth playing games again? Is he a ventriloquist? Who do I know who is given to that sort of coughing? Riyah. "I always cough in enclosed spaces," he had said. But why would he be in Hemsworth's dressing room? Did they know each other before they met at Scotland Yard? It didn't seem like it. I am jumping to conclusions. For goodness sake, all human beings cough at one time or another. And maybe it was, indeed, just a magician's little game. But if it wasn't . . . then that cough came from someone in hiding, someone listening . . . just like the first time we came here.

Irene is already well down the hallway, which is still lined with a dozen or more celebrated people hoping to have brief audiences with His Highness. She has only been off his arm for a few seconds, it seems, when she is engrossed in a conversation with a young man. He is there with another about his age, both dressed in elegant evening clothes. Sherlock looks down at his own slightly worn suit. He recognizes the gentleman – an actor, a rising star. His mustache is expertly waxed. He is strikingly handsome, known for his way with words, his burgeoning talent, and his interest in young ladies. Irene is touching him on the arm now, laughing at something he has said and smiling at the other young man too.

Sherlock brushes by them and heads down the hallway toward the street. *This is the way it will always be with Irene*

Doyle. Why do I deceive myself? He reaches the door. A young woman in her late teens is entering. *Very attractive*, he says to himself. Without thinking, he eyes her up and down, and then realizes what he is doing. Feeling guilty and aware of his own frailties, his thoughts return to Irene, and are more charitable. *She has every right to talk to those young men, just as I am allowed to notice other young ladies. If I believe that I should pursue my ambitions, shouldn't I believe that she can too? I should admire her. She is a good person . . . but she's of a different class than I am. I have to face it. Irene Doyle can't be for me.*

He shoves open the outside stage door at the back of the theater and walks at a brisk pace toward Piccadilly Street. He has his head down, his mind still on Irene, instead of on the fact that Alistair Hemsworth seems suddenly, and unfortunately, to be a suspicious character. The boy has even stopped thinking about his role in freeing him.

"Sherlock?"

Holmes looks up. Someone has picked him out of the crowd at the front of the theater, as if she were waiting for him. Two sparkling black eyes are looking his way.

"Beatrice!"

She is like a vision at this moment. Uninterested in the fancy-dressed people and handsome young men hailing cabs near her – some of whom look at her full figure with interest – she has a different focus. She is staring . . . at him.

"Just the man I was looking for."

"It is nice to see you."

"It is?"

"Yes."

Her face turns red. "Thank you. That is . . . What I meant to say was . . . I went to the shop to find you and Mr. Bell said you were 'ere. I was 'oping to meet again tomorrow and then visit your father . . . with you. I thought it might be easier if we went together. I know you said that you'd go yourself, but I spoke to 'im today and 'e said 'e 'adn't seen you, so I thought I'd call. I'm sorry if this is an imposition, but I thought I should try, because I –"

"Because you care?"

"Yes . . . I do."

"I should see him. You are right. And not some time in the distant future. Tomorrow. Are you at your work then?"

"Yes . . . but I can get someone to do my duties in the morning. Of course I can. Shall we meet, say, first thing, near Father's shop and take an omnibus. I can pay."

"That won't be necessary."

Sherlock crosses London Bridge early the following morning and stops by Snowfields School to tell the headmaster that his father is ill and he will not be able to lead his summer class until past noon. Then he makes his way, very slowly, to the Mint area, the south-of-the-river neighborhood where he used to live with his parents in a little flat above the Leckies' hat shop. Ratfinch, the fishmonger, slouching along with his barrels of eels in his cart is surprised to see him, and even more taken aback that his suit, so carefully brushed and tended to, is now just secondhand. But Sherlock doesn't respond to his greeting. In fact, he doesn't even look up to the small window above the shop when he arrives, but fixes his eyes on Beatrice, who is spotlessly dressed this morning too, all in red and veritably shining, a recently purchased matching bonnet on her head, looking as if she has scrubbed herself all night. She slips her arm through his, secretly happy, and he hails an omnibus to travel the three or four miles south to the Crystal Palace where Wilberforce Holmes tends to his beloved birds and white doves.

Every time the boy visited his father as a child, often hand in hand with his mother, the excitement began to build even before he left home. The glorious innards of the gigantic palace of entertainment awaited them: historical displays, circus acts, choirs, and maybe, just maybe, a sweet, a flavored ice, or a drink. It would be his treat for a whole season. They had always walked, and he had always waited for that moment when he would spy the great, nearly transparent building, still a mile or more away up on Sydenham Hill.

It is a gray day, and rain threatens. The boy is up on the knifeboards of the omnibus's roof, bare-headed, as usual, among the excited crowd of well-hatted, working- and middle-class men, dressed for the rain. Beatrice sits inside with the ladies, wondering what Sherlock is thinking. He doesn't look up to see the palace until they have pulled into the area around the train terminus at the south end of the park.

The rain has begun by the time they have made their way through the expansive grounds, past the sculptures of the lizard-like dinosaurs, the fountains, the athletic fields, and up the grand stone staircase to the front doors. Sherlock pays the entrance fee for Beatrice too, his coins nearly all gone now.

There aren't many visitors today, few excursionists coming from the country, since it is a weekday with poor weather. In his youth, Sherlock would always spot his father from the entrance and get permission from his mother to run to him through the thick crowds. Wilber Holmes was always particularly active by that time of the day, watching over his birds, readying things for that moment when he would release the hundreds of white doves of peace. He would turn to his son at the last moment, somehow magically knowing he was approaching, open his arms wide and hoist him into the air, before spinning him like a top. Sherlock never laughed more than during those moments. And when the spinning had stopped, Mr. Holmes would turn to Rose, his face lighting up, before she was enveloped in his arms too.

Today, Sherlock can't see his father at first, even though the crowds are sparse. Finally, he spots him, and sees why it took a while. Wilberforce is sitting down, and his appearance is shocking. He looks thin indeed, almost skeletal, and his big, black beard is streaked with gray.

Sherlock gasps. Beatrice takes him by the hand and brings him forward.

"Father?"

Wilber looks up. His ashen face brightens. His son had wondered if he might scowl, begin shouting, and tell him to leave.

"Sherlock? Is it really you?" Mr. Holmes gets to his feet and embraces the boy. For several seconds, he tries to lift him and spin him around, but he can't. So, he is happy to just hold his son's face and look into his eyes. "I miss you."

"I miss you too."

Beatrice steps back from them.

They say nothing for a few moments, then Mr. Holmes motions for Sherlock to sit beside him. "Thank you for your letters."

"It was my pleasure."

"I am delighted, you know, as I believe I once mentioned in a note, that you are dedicating yourself to justice. It makes me very happy. It would have pleased your mother as well."

For an instant, Sherlock can't speak. But he gathers himself. "You don't think it is just a childish dream?"

"Ambition is a desirable thing, if it is in the service of good. Remember that."

"I . . . I want us to see each other more often, Father."

"I would like that. And I would like to help you pursue this dream of yours."

"Catching criminals is really just science of a sort, isn't it?"

"Absolutely!"

The boy beams.

"Perhaps, Sherlock . . . perhaps we needed some time apart."

"I think you are right, sir."

"Well . . . let us imagine, my son, that nothing terrible ever happened, that we are just meeting again after a day or two, or perhaps your mother and I were just out for a long walk." Wilber has to pause for a moment, then continues. "Let us converse as we used to. So . . . I want to know what you are doing, right now, this week. Let's talk about that. What is occupying your time? What is on your mind?"

"A case, Father."

"A case! Tell me!"

Sherlock does. He tells him everything. When he is done, the elder Holmes is left rubbing his beard.

"This Riyah fellow. He said he was a Jew?"

"Yes."

"Did you ever notice, Sherlock, that I never actually called you a Jew? I never quite put it that way."

"No, sir."

"Well, I never did, and that was for a reason. You know me to be very particular about the things I say, very scientific?"

Sherlock grins. "Yes, Father."

"Well, you are not a Jew."

"Pardon me?"

"Not strictly. One only calls oneself a Jew when one's mother is Jewish."

Sherlock's eyes grow large as he begins to understand what Wilber is driving at: Riyah, as the boy has just related, said that *only* his father was Jewish.

"You see!" remarks Mr. Holmes, suddenly looking much healthier. "You will recall how I told you to observe everything intently at all times and to always listen very carefully too."

"Yes, and I do, I always do."

"Well, I was listening to you, very carefully, when you recounted your conversation with this Riyah chap. He calls himself a Jew . . . but he isn't. And his *real* name is Abraham Hebrewitz? It might as well be plucked from the pages of a novel! I smell a rat."

"My nose has been detecting a similar odor."

"Your big nose," says Wilberforce, gripping his own.

Sherlock laughs. "Yes, my big Jewish nose!"

They spend more than an hour together. Wilber neglects his duties, though he doesn't seem to care. But when it is time to leave, after they have hugged and promised to talk again, many times a week, his father appears to begin shrinking in size again, his hair seems grayer, and his expression saddens.

Sherlock can't look back again as he leaves.

"I wonder," he says, and a tear rolls down his face, "if I'll ever see him alive again."

"Nonsense," says Beatrice.

"I will get him to a good doctor. No, I'll do better than that: I'll take him to Mr. Bell!"

"Next week, Sherlock: we'll talk to your father about it next week."

"We?"

"Well, if you don't want –"

"Yes, that would fine. The two of us: let's do it together."

He mentions his worries about the Nottingham case. She listens and appears concerned.

As Sherlock looks into her face, it becomes clear to him that he will be leaving the Crystal Palace with two realizations. First, that he could never have shed a tear in front of Irene Doyle, but had no trouble doing it with Beatrice, and secondly, that his brilliant father, who gave him all the tools he needed to do what he so desperately wants to do in life – to avenge his mother's murder many times over, until the day he dies – has hit upon something that he himself suspected: there is something not quite right about Oscar Riyah. And that deeply increases the suspiciousness of Alistair Hemsworth. *Have I, because of my desire to impress a young lady, been the instrument of releasing a murderer? And what if this murderer has further horrors up his sleeve?*

BELL CHIMES IN

Sherlock has been to see one of his fathers, now he needs to talk to the other. He wakes the following morning, thinking of what they must discuss. It is a Thursday. He doesn't teach summer school classes this day of the week, and Bell is usually already out the door by now, visiting clients, so the boy expects to get some work done around the shop. He'll talk to his master after Big Ben strikes noon. But as he gains consciousness, Holmes hears the old man fussing about in the laboratory, knocking over torts and flasks, and banging impatiently on powders as he works with his mortar and pestle. It is obvious, from all this racket, that the alchemist is experimenting. When Sigerson Bell has a chemical idea he is like a dog worrying a meaty bone. He hears nothing and sees nothing, except his ideas and the components – the chemicals or alkaloids – he is mixing and matching. Sherlock hears him gently cursing in his polite manner and knows his master's mind is tightly engaged and far away.

Holmes quietly opens one of the doors of his wardrobe and peeks out. There is Bell across the room, facing his work, humming a violin concerto, punctuating it with a few of those benign but deeply-felt oaths.

"Horse manure!"

"Sir?"

Bell's head swivels around as if his neck were made of rubber. When it comes to rest, it seems to almost be on backwards. There is a look of horror on his face, as if he has been interrupted while performing a very personal act. The boy can see two huge flasks about five feet apart and between them all sorts of tubes and little homemade turbines and burning Bunsen lamps. Something is being turned to liquid in one flask and impelled toward the other at tremendous speed under white-hot pressure. There are rocks and powders and a couple of croaking frogs nearby, obviously the items he is attempting to transform into something else. At this very moment there is an explosion. It shakes the shop and all the equipment in front of the alchemist smashes and is propelled toward the ceiling. The force of the explosion is so great that the old man is slammed backward, landing at Sherlock's feet.

It takes everything a few seconds to settle.

"Sir, are you all right?"

The old man climbs to his feet and shoves his assistant to the side. In three or four bounds he is back at the scene of his experiment, holding something in his hand. It is glowing. It looks like gold.

"Eureka!" Bell shouts and begins to perform a jig. He turns, takes Sherlock by the hands, and dances with him too, then suddenly stops, looking guilty.

"Sir? What is it? What have you done?"

"Oh . . . nothing." He takes the material in his hand and holds it behind his back.

"That looks like a nugget of gold."

"Gold! . . . Nonsense! What are you accusing me of, sir!" He is attempting to sound angry, but it isn't very convincing.

"Have you transformed something into gold?"

"That . . . would be magic! That would be a ground-breaking, earth-shattering, God-like feat, a wondrous event in the history of mankind to be cherished by all who live upon our green earth, and would make the man who did it a living legend, though he would be expected to be humble about it, regardless of the fact that it would be, as I've noted, an unparalleled feat . . . so . . . no, sir, I have not done that of which you speak!" He turns quickly, rushes to a shelf, sets the material in his strongbox, and locks it.

"But sir –"

"Do we not have a lesson today? Violin? Chemistry? Bellitsu?"

"Yes, sir, but really, I just wanted to talk."

"Talk! By all means, let us talk!" He pulls up a chair and motions for Sherlock to sit at the table, then secures a stool for himself and lights upon it, putting his chin in his hands and looking lovingly at the boy. "Commence!"

"It's about Hemsworth."

"Ah, yes, we spoke briefly of him yesterday. Are you sure he is innocent? The question worries me, you know."

"It does?"

"Yes."

"Me too."

"Ah . . . thus, our chat?"

"You know I looked into it. All I wanted to do was investigate the crime scene and provide some evidence that might help Hemsworth before the magistrates, since it seemed, at first, that he may not have committed the crime. It did not appear fair that he should hang. I wanted to keep a distance from events, like you know I've been trying to do lately, even after I found some things at the scene that might help him. But Irene –"

"Ah!"

"And Beatrice –"

"Aha!"

"Please, sir, do not 'Aha!' me upon that subject."

"Yes, my boy, I am sorry."

"Miss Leckie was merely interested, merely helpful. Miss Doyle, whom you know convinced me to become involved in the first place, went further. She felt, after I returned from the scene, that we were close to truly helping Hemsworth . . . so I investigated more. Now I am concerned that I went further than I should have."

"Because it was due to your thorough intervention that His Highness was freed."

"Yes."

"Indeed, you should have been sure about this before you went to the police, and not listening to feminine types capable of swaying you. Hemsworth had a great deal of motivation to commit this crime, my boy, did he not? One cannot get over that, despite any circumstantial evidence to the contrary. I have heard rumors for many years that he is a little, shall we say, wild, a little loony, a cup and saucer short of a full tea set; that he is even cruel, at times, to others. Perhaps something happened to him on one of his many journeys? I am sure you are learning about him too. He is not a very nice man, is he?"

"No, sir, he doesn't seem to be, and he appears to have secrets."

"Well, he is a magician . . . though of the theatrical, sleight-of-hand sort, not a real one."

"I beg your pardon?"

"He doesn't know real magic."

"Like those who . . . turn substances into gold?"

"You, my boy, are far too clever for your own good," replies Bell angrily.

"I am sorry, sir."

Bell sighs and then grins. "Do not be. Pressure me! Seek the truth! Put my rear end to the wall, young man, press my buttocks against –"

"I will, sir, but not today. I need to know, now, what to do about this."

"You have little choice but to do *something*."

"Yes, sir, I wish I could leave it alone, but I am afraid that I have made a terrible mistake. I am at a loss as to where to start. I have already been to the crime scene – twice. That may have served only to lead me in the wrong direction. I have also been told, in no uncertain terms, never to go back there. It will be closely guarded from now on."

"Hmm. Here we have Hemsworth, the man who appears to have done it, the perfect candidate, anyway . . . but nothing to tie him to it."

"And no body."

"Yes, that is curious, my boy. Did Nottingham just vanish? You saw the scene. Were there really just his spectacles, blood, and bits of flesh, there? Is that all that was left of him?"

"Yes, that was all. How do you make someone disappear like that, master?"

"More than just some *one*. Mrs. Nottingham has vanished as well, has she not?"

They both think for a moment.

"Sir, do you really believe that you can transform substances into gold? If you can do that, couldn't someone, using real magic, make a human being disappear?"

"I believe that anything is possible. Anything! You know that. I teach you that, my boy! We are turning *you* into gold!"

"But do you think Hemsworth made Nottingham vanish? I mean *really* vanish."

"I think you are barking up the wrong tree . . . though you may be in the forest."

"I don't follow you."

"I might have believed *Nottingham* could make someone disappear. He was a clever man, that one. But I don't think Hemsworth is that good. He would use a slightly more down-to-earth method, shall we say. Did you notice anything unusual at the crime scene, anything really strange? Did you have any sense that something bizarre was concocted there?"

"Well, you know, sir, from the papers, about Mr. Riyah, who owns the hotel? I believe he was noted briefly in yesterday's news."

"Yes?"

"I found him in an inner chamber."

"An inner chamber? Well . . . that's not terribly surprising, I suppose. Whether this studio was let to Hemsworth or Nottingham, magicians like that sort of thing. Intrigue and mystery, you know!"

Suddenly something dawns on Sherlock. "But there was another place down there."

"Another place?"

"A second chamber, deeper under the building . . . and . . . and I heard noises coming from it . . . like something was alive down –"

Sigerson Bell stands bolt upright. "The dragon!"

"It couldn't be, sir."

"You saw it onstage! How real did it look? How real!?"

"You don't think . . . something like *that* killed the Wizard of Nottingham?"

The old man's eyes are on fire.

"I don't know, my boy, but if something like *that* did . . . it devoured him too."

FANTASTIC POSSIBILITIES

Sherlock is barely able to control Sigerson Bell after that. Just as Lestrade had seemed like he might explode during the great hat scene at Scotland Yard, the old apothecary looks like he might combust into a thousand bits and pieces. He leaps to his feet and literally begins running around the shop.

"If he has a dragon, then you need to find it. *We* do! Now *this* would intrigue me! Go out there, my boy, and slay that beast!"

"Slay it?"

"Well . . . find it, sir. Find it!"

"But I can't go back to The World's End Hotel."

"It is seen every other evening, you imbecile!"

Bell suddenly realizes what he has said. He apologizes profusely. He keeps on and on at it, pleading that he is just "unnaturally excited," until Sherlock feels as though he would like to apply a little Bellitsu to him to shut him up. Besides, the boy may be insecure about a number of things, but his intelligence is not one of them. He is not only aware that he is a sort of genius, but he believes it deeply and understands that such confidence is a great weapon in his arsenal.

"Sir, you must stop apologizing! I was being an imbe-cile indeed . . . on that particular point." Sherlock actually reaches out and seizes the old man, who has continued to run around the lab, talking.

"Yes. Yes, you were." He is breathing heavily.

"But you err slightly about my next move. There are actually *two* subjects that must be explored."

"Two? Ah! You have a plan! Now you are thinking, now you are rubbing those big spongy brain sections together! Let's see. The dragon, or whatever it is, must be found. And . . . and what?"

"Mrs. Nottingham must be located. I have a feeling she is playing a role in this. And it has just occurred to me how I might discover her whereabouts."

"Excellent! Shall you be attending the theater this evening? There is a show every other night, is there not?"

"No, I won't be attending."

"No?" Bell's face falls.

"*We* shall. I will speak to Irene and get us *three* tickets."

"Oh!" Sigerson Bell looks like he is about to collapse in tears. He throws his arms around the boy and nearly squeezes the life out of him. When Sherlock looks him in the face, a big tear is about to plop out. The old man pivots and scur-ries up the spiral stairs to his room. "I must dress for the evening. Simply in need of dressing, that's all!"

And what an outfit he is wearing at the theater that night. He is dressed, almost from head to foot, in pink. Sherlock had no idea he had such clothing – a billowing robe that looks vaguely Egyptian in style, worn, no doubt, to fit the décor of the theater. His red fez is, of course, upon his head. He has often told Sherlock that he has Egyptian fore-bears, going by the name of Trismegistus, and these clothes look like they may have belonged to them . . . several thousand years ago.

Irene, who is immaculately arrayed in a stunning gold dress (with tasteful bustle) that almost matches her hair, is never concerned about being seen with her social inferiors and doesn't even bat an eye when Sigerson Bell appears in his strange costume. She kisses him on the cheek, in continental style, and smiles. Sherlock has noticed that she is always excited to come to the theater, no matter how many times she attends. And this, of course, is His Highness's show, which she soon hopes to grace.

The performance is much the same as on other nights. All except for the presence of Bell, who has the irritating habit of commenting out loud and is often shushed by others around him. Like Sherlock, he sees through every trick and understands instantly how it is done. But when the dragon feat begins, he grows silent. He leans forward in his seat, breathing his fishy, garlic breath on the lady in front of him, but unaware of her discomfort, mesmerized by the beast on the stage. When it is done, he is left exhausted. Sherlock and Irene nearly have to pick him up.

"It looks real, my boy. It looks *real!* Don't you think?"

"He is just very clever, sir," says Irene.

"But he isn't, Miss Doyle. He isn't."

Bell and Sherlock have made plans to slip down the alleyway behind the theater after the show and wait outside to see Hemsworth come out and spot what he might bring with him. They arrived early for the production and discovered a large, stable-like door at the back, obviously used for over-sized stage props and the live animals that are often seen on this London stage. Now, they put Irene into a hansom cab and rush to the rear of the building.

As they wait in the shadows, Sherlock tells the old man more about how he freed Hemsworth. But Bell doesn't even smile at the Scotland Yard hat scene.

"The oldest trick in the book," he says glumly.

"Trick?"

"All magicians hats are adjustable, my boy. After all, they have to pull rabbits out of them, don't they?"

This doesn't make Sherlock feel any better as they wait.

Other than the musicians, there are only two people in the show. The first comes out a few minutes later. She is dressed plainly and wearing a veil, looking very different than she did onstage. Holmes steps from the shadows and walks up to her.

"Good evening," he says nonchalantly.

"Good evening, sir," she answers, but then gasps, puts her hand over her mouth, and rushes off.

"Who was that?" asks Bell.

"A lady who has just agreed to tell me all she knows about Mrs. Nottingham, though she isn't aware of it yet."

Within seconds, Hemsworth, with no dressing-room visits tonight, leaves the building too. Sherlock and Bell move deeper into the shadows. But there is nothing to see. The magician simply walks up the alley to the front of the theater and Piccadilly Street, gets quickly into a waiting hansom cab, and is gone. The apothecary and his apprentice follow at a distance.

"Where's the dragon?" asks Bell.

"The dragon? Or the illusion? Perhaps there is nothing to find."

Sherlock is looking up Piccadilly, but not following Hemsworth's cab. His eyes are on the foot pavement.

"I have something I need to do, sir. I will meet you back at the shop."

Sherlock is watching the disappearing figure of the lady with the veil, walking away in the now-sparse crowd, looking back over her shoulder. Without waiting to hear Bell respond, he runs after her. She has a good two-hundred-foot start on him. But he closes the gap quickly. She knows he is pursuing, but doesn't seem to want to be conspicuous, so she doesn't take to her heels. Instead, she moves as fast as she can at a walk. At the first side street, she turns south. It is a small, winding artery with almost no one on it and here, she begins to run. Sherlock can't believe how fast she is moving. *Can women really run like this?* But she is in a dress and wearing heels, and by the time she gets to a little park at St. James Square, he has reached her. They are alone now. She turns to face him. This is a brave young lady.

"How did you know to speak to me?" She pulls her veil back, revealing a face as black as Beatrice's servant's uniform. She looks defiant. They are both breathing heavily.

"I observe, Miss Venus."

"It isn't Miss."

Every time the boy has been to see the Hemsworth show he has watched the magician's exotic "African" assistant closely. His Highness presents her as a native beauty he captured on the Dark Continent, unable to understand English, though trained to obey his commands . . . Venus of the Hottentots. At the end of each night, still wearing her nearly see-through linen costume, but by then under a purple robe, she is magically transformed into a fair-skinned princess . . . and placed in the cage with the dragon. It is a spectacular effect.

"Just Venus?"

"I am not deemed fit to have a title."

"What is your real name?"

"What do you want?"

"Some answers."

"I am unable to supply them. Good evening." She drops her veil again and turns to leave.

"I shall go to the press – *The News of the World* would be fascinated – and let them know that you are from . . . where is it . . . Brixton?"

She gasps, stops, turns back, and lifts the veil again.

"How . . . how do you know that? How did you know I spoke English in the first place?"

"Well, I had to confirm it by greeting you this evening. But as for the rest, let's say that details are important to me. I studied you onstage. I noticed that whenever he made an error, which was often, he would speak to you under his breath. He didn't motion, he spoke, and you responded with your actions. It was obvious that you could understand him. And you have a Brixton accent, northern part, is it, second or third generation? I make it my business to know such things."

"But you are just a boy. Of what intrigue is this to you? Is someone paying you? Is this just to cause a scandal in the Sunday papers?"

"I have an interest in the Nottingham murder. Tell me what I need to know and I shall keep your secret."

"An interest? On which side? Solving the case . . . or were you involved in committing it?" She steps back from him.

"My proposition is simple. I repeat: tell me what I need to know . . . and I will keep your secret."

She hesitates. ". . . My name is Juliet. I won't tell you my last, unless you force me. I was raised in Brixton, yes, my grandfather was a slave, but my father was in the service, a footman in Belgravia. My brothers and I were educated. But I was a restless youth, didn't want to work for others. What could a Negro woman do? I was strong and fearless, I could actually compete at athletics with my brothers . . . and I was pretty. In the circus arts, they don't care about the color of your skin because they can use it. My appearance made me exotic and alluring. I learned to ride a horse and do tricks, I learned the trapeze. I wore few clothes in my performances and became a favorite among the men. A nearly-naked black woman isn't as scandalous as a white one . . . but it has the same effect."

"Zaza? You are Mademoiselle Zaza?"

"I was."

"You hurt your back, didn't you? That accident at the Royal Amphitheatre? I thought you simply retired."

"Performers don't retire at twenty-one, young man. I disappeared. They couldn't use me after my fall. I was almost on the streets when Hemsworth found me. I was perfect for him. He pays me more than I could make anywhere else, and it's just our two names on the program. You cannot tell anyone that I am not who he says I am! I need this job, sir. What do you want?"

"As I said, just answers. How long have you been with him?"

"About two years, I'd say. I suppose I am just as exotic in his act as I was in my own. I am still wearing very few clothes. It keeps the gentlemen interested when His Highness fumbles."

Two years. When did Nottingham steal his wife away?

"Did you know Mrs. Nottingham when she was Hemsworth's wife?"

"Oh, yes. I was there when she seduced the Wizard. She went right for him and bagged him."

"Seduced Nottingham?"

"Everyone thinks it was the other way around. Women don't do such things. She was a nice lady though. She was good to me. Not many in her position would be. She treated me as an equal; it was remarkable. But she liked fame and she liked men. She wasn't a looker, but she wasn't unattractive either, and she had a spirit about her, an accommodating one, shall we say, that men couldn't resist. Nottingham certainly couldn't, though I think he later wished he could have.

In the end, it was helpful for both magicians, though. It gained them a great deal of attention in the newspapers. Both men exploited that part, at least at first."

"What is Hemsworth like?"

"He is a beast. All he cares about is his show. . . . He hits me . . . but he pays me well. He says horrible things about his former wife, vile things about how he would kill her in gruesome ways if he could, after what she did to him. Nottingham wasn't much better to work for, I hear. He was very ambitious. People in his show say he would sell his soul to the devil for a great trick, one as amazing as the dragon illusion."

"Have the police spoken to you?"

"To Venus, the half-clothed, illiterate African beauty? They looked at me, they did, just like other men. But no, they haven't asked me anything, and I would prefer, sir, if you would be so kind, to keep it that way."

"I will if you answer one more question and tell me the truth. Do you have any idea where Mrs. Nottingham is?"

"I do."

"You do?" Sherlock's heart races.

"She started coming back to Hemsworth's shows a few months ago, when they became a great sensation. She loved to be where the action was, where all the celebrated people were. I noticed her sitting with men from the continent on several nights: handsome, wealthy ones. She couldn't resist them. His Highness told me, just last week, that she ran off with one of them. I don't know why he bothered to tell me, perhaps he was gloating. I don't think he has told anyone else, at least he doesn't seem to have informed the police. He knows I don't speak much to others."

"She's run off?"

"I doubt it was meant to be permanent, probably just one of her affairs. But she won't come back now, why would she? Especially since Hemsworth is free. Her husband vanishes and so does she. With no one accused of the crime now, she could very well be a suspect, couldn't she?"

"Yes, she could. You're in the business – why do you think Nottingham didn't tell anyone?"

"Because he has the same pride as Hemsworth. It isn't just a male tendency, though that is bad enough. They can't ever look like failures to the public. He was probably hoping he could keep her flight quiet and she would come back. Perhaps she has done it before."

"And you say Hemsworth hasn't told the authorities where she's gone," muses Sherlock out loud.

"Maybe he liked being a suspect for a while."

"Liked it?"

"It was good for business, wasn't it? He is always thinking about that. His arrest caused a sensation. I always had the feeling that he knew they couldn't convict him."

"Well, they will, if I have anything to do with it."

"They will? I am not so sure, young man. I despise Hemsworth, but I'm not certain that he did it. He isn't clever enough to pull off a perfect crime. And as for his hating Nottingham, I'm not even convinced about that."

"But –"

"I'm not saying that His Highness wasn't angry and resentful after his wife left – I know he was. But I think he blamed her more than the Wizard. Their rivalry may have been a bit of a dressed-up thing, like many things in show business, something they used. I saw the two of them talking just a few days before the murder, behind the theater. They didn't seem upset, though they stepped away from each other when they saw me."

"Miss Juliet, it is not unusual for a villain to stalk his prey in order to discover what he is up to. Perhaps Hemsworth was pretending to be past his anger . . . as he plotted. Maybe he was inviting the Wizard into his lair and you simply witnessed him drawing him in."

"I hadn't thought of that." Her beautiful face looks frightened. "That gives me the shivers."

"What about the dragon? You've seen it up close. Is it real?"

"I don't know. I don't really see it onstage. Can I go? I've answered everything you asked. I can't afford to be seen on the street talking to anyone." She pulls her veil down again.

He waves her off and she rushes away.

"*I don't really see it onstage.*" It is a curious statement. *But she is blindfolded at that moment, of course. She is probably the only one in the theater who doesn't see it. And Hemsworth is so secretive that she likely never so much as glimpses it any other time. But can't she feel its presence in the cage during those terrifying seconds, sense if it is real or not, smell its very breath? She was so calm when she spoke of it. That seems awfully strange. . . . Or is it? Maybe it's proof that the dragon isn't real, that it is all just a trick? Or is Venus simply a consummate professional, a steely nerved former daredevil?*

Whatever the case, Holmes thinks again, in admiration of how Hemsworth disguises Juliet as a white woman for that scene, how he transforms her. *It must be makeup and lights.* It is perfect: it serves to not only fill the audience with wonder, but scare them even more . . . a white woman in grievous peril. He may not be the greatest magician, but he is an extraordinary showman. He knows what thrills London.

Tonight, Sherlock has found an important piece of the puzzle, or at least, helped eliminate one. He now knows where Mrs. Nottingham has gone, and that he cannot pursue her – he doesn't have the resources to find her on the continent, and obviously, she is interested in staying lost. He has just one option left, the one he discussed with Sigerson Bell. He must find out what instrument of terror Hemsworth used to reduce Nottingham to tiny specs of flesh . . . he must explore the possibility that it was a living and breathing monster, a Frankenstein beast.

And whatever it was . . . and is . . . he must hunt it.

DESPERATION

That night he dreams of slaying a dragon. He stands before it wearing Saint George's armor, bearing the ancient red-crossed flag of England, his sword drawn. The creature looms over him, monstrous in size, forked tongue darting out. Defeating it seems an impossible quest. A crowd, led by Inspector Lestrade, has come up the hill from a nearby village and gathers around. They wield weapons and offer their help. But Sherlock must do this alone. He sees Irene and Beatrice looking on, and Scuttle bursting with pride, telling the others in the crowd that he knows him. When Sherlock is done, they will all cheer and his fame will be sung throughout the kingdom. He turns to the beast . . . and it kills him.

Holmes rises the next morning thinking that he must visit his father again. He puts it off. He will go to school first. But all day in the classroom he feels guilty. Guilt is coming at him from so many sources: he isn't visiting his father and he may very well be responsible for setting free a murderer, making it possible for the villain to act again. On top of everything, Sherlock isn't offering the police his latest evidence . . . proof that he may have erred.

When he thinks of his father he thinks of something he was taught long ago.

"I am going to teach you about a word, son," Wilberforce once said. "That word is *integrity*. It has to do with honesty, but it is much more than that. It is about never lying to yourself, never doing what you know is wrong, making sure that what you say you believe in is what you do. I want you to always be a man of integrity."

"Integrity?" Sigerson Bell remarked earlier this year, when Sherlock, feeling a little homesick, brought up the subject. "It is the chief characteristic of a great man. If you do not exhibit it while in my employ I shall plunge it into you like a sailor dropping an anchor into the sea, hammer it into you like a spike being drilled into your skull, like a surgeon reaching into your chest and carving your heart out whilst it is still beating and showing it to you, blood still pumping from –" Then he realized he had gone too far, and commenced to apologize. It lasted for a week.

Sherlock Holmes knows he is not a young man of integrity at this moment. He had felt it most acutely this morning while instructing his summer students on the subject of History, and what has been, over the centuries, right . . . and wrong. His late August classes finish at two o'clock. He has time to do what is right today. When school ends, and after more soul searching, he finds his way . . . to Scotland Yard.

This is one of the most difficult things he has ever had to do. He paces up and down Whitehall Street before summoning the courage to enter the police offices. He knows that Lestrade Sr. won't see him, so he asks for his son. The young detective appears, reluctantly.

"I am surprised that you would show your face here."

"I was . . . not correct," Sherlock blurts out. "I *may* have not been correct."

"I beg your pardon?"

"I may have been . . . wr . . . wr . . . wrong."

"Wrong? Did you say you were *wrong* about something? Can you repeat that?"

"I was wrong."

"And again?"

"Lestrade!"

The other boy laughs. But he doesn't when Sherlock tells him what he is concerned he's wrong about.

"You think Hemsworth is guilty?! You, who are responsible for setting him free! Father!"

The desk sergeant nearly jumps from his seat.

"*May* be guilty, I said *may* be. Don't call your father . . . I can't face –"

"FATHER!"

The Senior Inspector is in the foyer in seconds. He doesn't hear his son shout at him with such volume often and is concerned that something is terribly wrong.

"Son?" Then he sees Sherlock. "The Holmes brat! Get him out of here!"

"Father, he has something to tell you, something you are going to be very interested to hear."

"That's impossible."

"No, sir, it isn't." He turns to Sherlock and motions to him, as if handing him the stage.

Sherlock can barely speak at first. He starts slowly but picks up speed. Lestrade seethes as he listens, his face growing progressively more red. The boy tells him that he is worried that his solution to the Hemsworth question was too easy, that he is feeling guilty about it, that all that motivation is still very much against the magician, that he has learned of His Highness's cruelty and immorality, that Hemsworth may very well have been acting during the hat scene, that all magicians keep adjustable hats (Lestrade almost cries out at this), that Mr. Riyah isn't really a Jew though he claims to be, that his real name is under suspicion, that someone was hiding in Hemsworth's dressing room both times he and Miss Doyle visited, that it may have been Riyah, that he worries that those two men have known each other for some time but pretend to be strangers and –

"ENOUGH!" shouts Lestrade.

Sherlock closes his mouth.

"You are a fool, do you know that? A boob!"

"Yes, sir."

"You have put us into a great conundrum! Through your interference, you have freed the man whom I have known from the start to be the murderer. You have provided him with an alibi. But now, you have gathered circumstantial evidence that veritably *proves* my theory!"

"Circumstantial?"

"None of what you say, though very telling and harmful to the reputations of a number of the principals . . . can hang the villain!"

"That is correct," adds the Inspector's son, grinning at Sherlock. "You were correct all along, sir, and you are correct now."

"Thank you, son." Lestrade turns on Sherlock again. "You have nothing that places Hemsworth at the crime scene. Your little hat demonstration took care of that! You do not have a murder weapon, or even any idea as to how it was done! And yet we *all*, even you, have come to the understanding that he did it." Lestrade begins furiously pacing around the foyer. "But *how* did he do it? It didn't matter before, when we had his hat inches from the blood, but now it does! Now we *must* know. Did Hemsworth blow him up? Did he wave a wand and make him vanish?"

"No sir. I doubt that."

"Then how?"

"I have a theory."

"A theory!!" shout the two Lestrades at once, both smirking.

"This," continues the Inspector, "should be enjoyable, a tale for the London stage." He stops moving about. "Perhaps we should sit down, serve tea? Go on. Enlighten us."

"Sir . . . what . . . if it wasn't a human being? What if the villain was another sort of creature? That might account for what was left behind."

"Not surprisingly, you aren't making sense."

"What if it was a beast?"

"A beast? Of what sort?"

"A dragon."

Young Lestrade laughs out loud. But his father does not. He turns and looks out the window. "A dragon?"

"Or whatever it is that Hemsworth has created to look like one."

"That's ridiculous," says young Lestrade.

"Have you been to see the show, sir?"

"Of course, we watched it the night we arrested him."

"And what did you think?"

Lestrade swallows. "To be honest . . . I found it . . . rather convincing."

"But it can't be a real dragon, Inspector, can it?"

"Of course not . . . that's nonsense."

"But there was nothing left of Nottingham . . . just his spectacles and blood . . . and little pieces of flesh. Can a human being do that?"

Lestrade swallows again. "I have long suspected that there is something magical about this crime. But –"

"Sir, it would be simple for you to either prove or eliminate this possibility. You have the power to stop the show at the moment the dragon appears."

Sherlock doesn't want to tell the Inspector about the third chamber below The World's End Hotel. He will hold that card up his sleeve. He has no idea what is down there anyway. At this point, the police are not even aware of the second room. If he were to send them on an investigation of the inner chambers and they found nothing of interest, he would look like an even greater fool than he appears now. *I know that this apparition, this dragon, appears on The Egyptian Hall stage at the end of every show. I don't know what is in that chamber. If I have to gamble, I should bet on the surer thing, what I have seen with my own eyes . . . we must seize this thing, whatever it is, red-handed, during the performance.*

"I cannot subject us to possible ridicule in front of an audience," snaps the Inspector.

"Then you could simply position yourselves backstage and keep the dragon from being secreted away again, as it somehow must be following each performance? You, sir, could examine His Highness Hemsworth's great illusion."

Lestrade looks tempted. He starts pacing again. "If the magician . . . has something, even a disguised lion or tiger, or a giant hound, then we might be able to, at least, keep the case against him in motion, put the circumstantial evidence together with him harboring a murderous beast capable of . . ." He comes to an abrupt halt and barks at the desk sergeant. "I want this Riyah fellow brought in!" He hesitates to give his next order.

"There is no show tonight, sir. Hemsworth performs every other evening. You could attend tomorrow."

Lestrade regards him for a moment, then turns back to the desk sergeant. "Get us some tickets to the next Egyptian Hall spectacle!" He glances at the boy. "Get one for him as well." Then, looking directly at Sherlock, he mutters, "This had better be worthwhile!"

On the street outside the station, Holmes has the feeling that someone is watching him. He scans the court in Scotland Yard and thinks he sees a dark face peering around a corner just two buildings away. He runs toward it, but by the time he arrives, it has flown, out into the heavy crowds on Whitehall Street. Sherlock squints and looks into the masses. He thinks he sees the man, wearing a black greatcoat, much like Riyah's.

The boy pauses in the majestic park in front of Buckingham Palace for a while on his way home, watching the swans in the queen's ponds. He decides to walk past The Egyptian Hall. It is a hot afternoon and the front doors are open. The boy can hear music and a beautiful voice. It sounds familiar. He walks up to the entrance. Someone is accompanying a woman on a piano, both the playing and the singing informal, like a rehearsal. The voice is familiar indeed. *Irene.* Then he hears a scream, a bloodcurdling shriek. He runs into the lobby, past a few attendants, who are lounging about and smoking. He rips open the doors of the amphitheater and comes to the top of the lower bowl. Irene Doyle is standing on the stage close to a piano, where Hemsworth sits playing. The magician rises.

"Master Holmes?"

"Sherlock?"

"Are you all right, Miss Doyle?"

"I am fine, Master Holmes."

The attendants enter and seize the boy from behind.

"Unhand him, gentleman," says Hemsworth. "I shall take care of this." The attendants slouch back to the lobby.

"But that scream . . ."

"It is a frightening show, my boy. Severed heads, live dragons?"

"We are working on a song, Sherlock. There may be," she smiles at Hemsworth, "a scream involved."

Holmes doesn't like that smile.

"I hear you are coming tomorrow, Holmes?"

"Where did you hear that?"

"Well, I am clairvoyant, you know. I read minds, tell the future, that sort of thing."

"Are you finished, Miss Doyle? Would you like me to accompany you home?"

Holmes hasn't had a chance to tell Irene about his suspicions. It also occurs to him that she might consider his visit to the police a betrayal, an interference that might destroy her great opportunity. He glances at Hemsworth, who grins back at him.

"We have just begun, Sherlock. You go on. I will see you later."

What if she is rehearsing with a murderer?

"Are you sure?"

"Please go."

Holmes doesn't return to the apothecary shop. He walks toward Irene's Bloomsbury neighborhood, thinking about all the evidence he has accumulated. Circumstantial or not, it is compelling. Both Lestrades are sure who did it. *Hemsworth is no fool. He must know that I know. I could tell by the way he looked at me. How on earth does he know we are coming tomorrow night?* The boy reaches Montague Street and waits near a side entrance to the British Museum, watching the front door of the Doyle home on the other side of the street. But he waits in vain. Irene doesn't appear. Just before midnight, he trudges home.

There is no sign of her on Montague Street the following morning before he goes to school to do some chores, or when he comes home about noon. He stays hidden across from her home for hours and she doesn't appear. He even tries her door, but it is locked. The Egyptian Hall entrance is secured, as well, and there is no sound coming from inside. *Perhaps I missed her . . . very late last night. Perhaps she went out this morning and stayed out all day.* He prays that it is true.

THE DRAGON AT THE EGYPTIAN HALL

Though Irene isn't scheduled to be part of the show that evening, Sherlock expects, and hopes, to see her in the audience. But when the boy picks up his ticket at the booth, he notices that her pass is unclaimed. As the lights go down, he is beside himself with worry. He squirms in his seat, hers empty next to his, his heart pounding. *Why do I involve her in my obsessions? Why can't I leave them alone until I am older, until I am truly equipped to make a difference? I should have learned by now, but I keep allowing myself to be drawn back to her, and she draws me to what I should not do. Has Hemsworth made her disappear, in the same way he disposed of Nottingham?*

He can't stand it anymore. He rises to his feet and roughly moves past seated spectators to the aisle. An usher spots him and approaches from behind. But he isn't planning to leave the theater: far from it. He is heading for the stage.

Hemsworth's erotic Far Eastern music has begun, played by the ten-piece band in the orchestra pit. The beguiling Venus is before the audience, alone, those bits of flimsy white muslin wrapped around her midsection, exposing her legs and her entire midriff, and barely covering her chest. Her dark skin glistens in the spotlight as she dances, beckoning the audience's attention toward her, making her way to stage right and a huge scimitar – an East Indian sword with a shining handle and long steel blade, devilishly turned up at the point. It is suspended in midair, where it will be the magician's weapon for his decapitation feat. She will grip it and caress it, before seductively motioning for the great man to enter from stage left. He will prostrate himself before her . . . and she will slice off his head.

Sherlock is running now. The attendant behind him can't catch up, and the other, the one next to the stage door, is taken by surprise. The boy rushes by and is instantly backstage. Here, one staircase leads down to the dressing rooms, the other up to the wings. He is just below stage left. He flies upward. There, stands Hemsworth, resplendently dressed in his white adventurer's outfit, trousers and shirt gleaming, big black boots and black safari hat framing him, about to make his entrance. He sees Sherlock coming toward him and, for some reason, simply smiles at him, and waves off the attendant who has followed. The boy will have none of that: he makes for His Highness, but the magician glides away, onto the stage. And as he does, someone is revealed behind him. *Irene.* Sherlock stops. She is watching from the wings too, relaxed and happy . . . until she sees Holmes. She looks at him with suspicion, sensing something unpleasant in his sudden backstage appearance. The boy drops his head and stands still and quiet. He stays that way throughout the entire first act.

During intermission, Hemsworth, his face lit up by the performance, eyes glittering as if he has ingested some of Sigerson Bell's cocaine concoctions, takes a moment to greet him.

"Master Holmes, I am so glad you could make it..I trust this spot is advantageous for spectating? You will have a unique view of my creature. I believe some friends of yours will be here as well?"

How does he know that? Sherlock wants to talk to Irene about Hemsworth, tell her his suspicions, but the magician takes her aside and keeps her from him.

Just as the second act begins, the stage door opens again and the Lestrades enter with a plainclothes policeman in tow. Though they had to flash their badges at the attendant, they are trying not to cause a fuss.

Irene looks from them to Sherlock, not pleased.

Once she sees the beast up close, sees what it is capable of, reconsiders what was left of Nottingham's body, and then hears what we know of His Highness and his secret relationship with Riyah, she will understand.

They all wait silently for the big moment, the dragon sensation. And when it comes . . . it disappoints.

The beast, seen from the wings of the theater, is obviously fake. It looks like it is made of papier mâché and its wings, its mouth, the long forked tongue, indeed move mechanically. *Its animated effect must be enhanced with mirrors and lighting!*

Hemsworth is all action as the stage dims. In the darkness, he is seen pulling the dragon illusion from the stage to a spot behind the curtains and, curiously, roughly pulling Venus away too. He vanishes behind the scenes with her for a moment and then returns to take the house's applause.

But from the wings, this audience doesn't look as impressed as the others were on previous nights. Then Hemsworth saves it all. He turns to his five onlookers at stage left: Lestrade and his sidekicks are about to leave inconspicuously out the back door.

"I must tell you," the magician booms to the audience in his deep baritone, "that tonight we have distinguished guests in our midst. The police, as you know, arrested me for the horrible murder of the Wizard of Nottingham, may he rest in peace." Lestrade stops in his tracks, a look of dread coming over his face. Onstage, Hemsworth removes his hat and holds it over his heart. "I am free now, as an innocent man should be." The crowd roars and he bows to them. "But," adds His Highness, "the Force cannot give it up. It seems, they still think something nefarious is at work in my mind and in my actions. So . . . they are here tonight! I ask you, to give them a magically gigantic ovation. Gentlemen?"

He motions for all three policemen to come onstage. They freeze. The applause builds. He motions to them again. "Don't be shy!"

They make their entrance, heads down.

"This is the famous Inspector Lestrade, he who erroneously arrested me." The crowd roars with laughter. "And this is his son, and this is one of his respected slaves." Another roar. "Find anything of interest tonight, gentlemen?"

Sherlock can't look. As he turns away, he notices Venus slipping past the door that leads backstage. She is rushing down the hall where the dressing rooms are situated. She has made a remarkably fast change from her white-woman-in-peril role. Her face is a beautiful ebony again, and she is already wearing her dress. He remembers that she was the first out the door when he accosted her two nights ago. *She mustn't want to be near Hemsworth any longer than necessary.*

Irene turns angrily to Sherlock. "You supported this, didn't you? You put them up to it? Why?"

"I think he is guilty. And I think you should stay away from him."

"Guilty? You set him free. *We* set him free."

"I am worried that we shouldn't have."

"Worried? What happened to evidence? Facts! Remember?"

"I tried to keep you informed. . . . Where were you all day?"

"We were rehearsing – it takes time. Listen, Sherlock, we are friends, better than friends. And I want it to stay that way. But you are *so* frustrating sometimes! I hope Hemsworth still wants me." She exits through the stage door and out of the theater.

Holmes would like to follow, slink away with her, but he knows he must face the music. If he doesn't, he will be summoned to Scotland Yard, anyway.

The Lestrades take him out into the alley, so no one can hear them. Sherlock has heard of police actually beating people, there are stories in *The News of the World* about it from time to time. Lestrade's face isn't red on this occasion, it is purple.

"Father, you must restrain yourself," says his son, holding on to him, but the Inspector slaps his hands away.

"You, mister-half-Jew-interfering-disgusting-lowlife brat, have ruined everything about this case! And my reputation with it!"

If only that were possible.

"I would have you shot if I could!"

"Sir, I don't think –"

"Shut your GOB, Master Lestrade!" The lad shrinks back.

"You, Holmes, are now old enough to be treated as an adult. You, sir, can have your reputation destroyed too!"

"Sir?"

"FIND ME THE DRAGON! That's all we have left!"

"What do you mean?"

"Here's your choice. . . . Find me a real, live dragon, and prove that Hemsworth used it to kill Nottingham . . . or I destroy your future! What do you think your chances are, half-breed? I have the power to end your dreams, and I am about to do it. I shall detail to the press, *detail*, how you have interfered with police affairs before. How *you* are the trickster behind freeing a man whom the entire Metropolitan London Police Force believes is the murderer of the nation's most popular showman!" He pauses, then shouts again, "I know what you want to do with your life, boy!"

"And so I shall." Sherlock sticks out his prominent chin.

"Not if the newspapers and the entire enforcement of authority in this city know that you plot the release of heinous criminals! Who will work with you then? Give you one ounce of help?" He turns to go, then comes back to the boy. "I could have your head this instant. I know you broke into The World's End Hotel – twice! What would that cost you before the magistrates? Five years? Ten? What would that cost your little career plans? You think you know something about this case? Prove it! You have hamstrung *us*!"

"How long do I have?"

"I may speak to the press tonight, perhaps tomorrow morning. Perhaps in two days. . . . Maybe three? I may *arrest* you at *any* time. You will *never* solve this! But I want you to squirm. I want you to wonder when the axe will fall, the guillotine . . . on your neck!"

"What . . . what about Mr. Riyah? If we could make him confess –"

"We have looked high and low for him! We had Hemsworth's dressing room searched. It is a single, sealed room, you fool! Mr. Riyah has vanished!"

He stomps off, taking the policeman with him. Only young Lestrade remains.

"Well, this should be simple enough, my friend," he remarks. "I'd say the odds are with you. All you have to do . . . is produce a dragon!"

S herlock walks back to the apothecary shop feeling frightened. *All I have to do is find a dragon? And do it with haste. Find a dragon, when I know now that the only one alive in England is an illusion, when I know that the entrance to The World's End inner chamber – which is likely empty – is guarded around the clock? I've done it again! I've put everything, this case and my whole future, in jeopardy!*

His mood isn't helped by the fact that he senses he is being followed again. But he can't see anyone at first. He walks up Piccadilly, through Leicester Square, and north toward Denmark Street. Once or twice, as he moves along, he thinks he glimpses his pursuer . . . a man in a black great-coat. *It must be my imagination.* But it makes him think. If Riyah isn't who he says he is, then who is he? Is the old "Jew" a dressed-up actor? Sherlock considers the man's size, the way he slips through the crowds so easily and undetected and knows the streets. Who would be good at that sort of thing? *Who might want to follow me and keep following?* Who has his hands on sensational criminal activity in London? Who would want to keep tabs on Sherlock Holmes, but remain hidden? He thinks of the pursuer's coat again and realizes that he has never seen it clearly. *Could it be a coat with tails?* A thought freezes him. *Malefactor!* But the boy shakes it off. *It couldn't be . . . could it?*

Back at the shop, Sherlock tells Bell everything that happened before he turns in. The old man shakes his head sadly at first, but then rubs his chin thoughtfully and retires upstairs. The boy tosses and turns in his little bed and can't sleep. The next day is Sunday. That's good – it isn't a day on which Lestrade is likely to act. He rises late and gives a street urchin two pennies to take a note to the home of Snowfields' headmaster, informing him that "due to circumstances beyond my control," he cannot teach summer classes for the next few days. He doesn't mention that he will be spending every minute of that time searching for a dragon.

He also sends an invitation to Irene Doyle: he needs to see her. She appears at teatime in mid afternoon. The day is hot and muggy, and she is wearing a blood-red dress with a parasol, her arms bare all the way from her elbows to her wrists, another outfit that would look perfect on a stage. *Dressed for Hemsworth*, thinks Sherlock. Bell has somehow gotten wind of Miss Doyle's invitation and has commenced to make them a rather sumptuous tea, complete with his best Indian brew poured into his best flasks, and scones seasoned with calf brains, a surprisingly tasty item, the ingredients of which are not revealed to Miss Doyle. The bent-over apothecary then returns up the spiral staircase to his room, though Sherlock spots him every now and then, peering at them through the opening in the floor.

"Thank you for having me," says Irene, taking a stool at the laboratory table. "Let us put last night behind us."

"Irene, I have a few things to tell you. First, you must know why I suspect Alistair Hemsworth."

"Speak as you please, but it won't change my mind."

He tells her, in detail. She keeps eating as he does, nodding from time to time at the remarkable flavor in the scones, but seemingly unaffected by the information.

"What kind of evidence do they call that?"

"Convincing?"

"No . . . circumstantial, isn't it? Evidence that doesn't really –"

"I know what it means, Irene."

A button comes bouncing down the staircase, one that Sherlock noticed was getting loose on Bell's laboratory smock this morning, but when they both look up, all they see is wispy white hair and the top of a bald head darting away.

"Why are you telling me this?" she asks.

"I want you to stay away from him. It would set my mind at ease while I, while I –"

"Pursue the case?"

"Well, it's what you are always pushing me to do."

"Not this time. You have done your work. Hemsworth is free."

"To do more mischief because of me; and I am free to be jailed or disgraced if I can't stop him."

"Sherlock, it *isn't* him. And it *isn't* some dragon. That is a lunatic idea. It is beneath you. You are allowing yourself to be obsessed, instead of using reason . . . as we always say we should do. Tell the police about Mrs. Nottingham. She is obviously not what she seemed . . . rather like your friend, Miss Leckie. Remember that women can be just as beastly as men. The Wizard's wife had reason to murder him. She is in love with someone else. Suddenly, she vanishes? She probably knows about her husband's secret studio. She may be the only other person who does. It fits. The way you found out about her was genius." She winks at him and he blushes. "Find her. Then figure out how *she* did it. Forget about chasing dragons."

"I can't betray Miss Juliet. I can't reveal her identity. She told me about Mrs. Nottingham in confidence."

"Then I will. I don't need to play the gentleman. We must do what is right. The police should know this. If it is her, and they can find her, you are off the hook too. Justice will be served, which is what matters in the end."

"Don't tell them. Give me a day or two. I don't think it's Mrs. Nottingham, anyway. How did she kill a grown man and leave behind just his spectacles, his blood, and pieces of his flesh?"

"You will always underestimate women, won't you?" She pauses. "I can't stand by and keep this information quiet. Neither should you. But I will give you a little time."

"You sound like Lestrade."

"Sherlock, he hates you. I . . . I like you, very much. I can see the day when you will be a great detective, and I will be singing at the Royal Opera House. What a couple we could be!"

She's right. A glorious future flashes through his mind, their fame riveting London as they live their dreams.

But then the boy hears his father's voice, reminding him to be practical at all times, to never be seduced by romantic notions. *No woman should marry a detective.* "I cannot allow you to have anything to do with Hemsworth. I cannot put you in danger again."

Irene's eyes narrow. "*Allow* me? Sherlock, I am not your slave, nor will I ever be. I will make my own decisions."

"Here, here!" says a loud whisper upstairs.

Sherlock glares upward. "I am going to prove that Hemsworth murdered his rival, the Wizard of Nottingham, and that this cowardly act was one of the most brutal in the annals of London crime."

"Good luck to you, then."

"I have no choice."

"You know, you may be wrong about that too. It might not be a bad thing if Lestrade revealed your part in all of this. Think about it. Even if it made you notorious, that might be good for you in the long run. I am beginning to believe that any publicity is good publicity."

"Wrong!" cries a high-pitched voice upstairs. Now Irene glares upward.

"Good morning, Miss Doyle," says Holmes and rises to his feet.

"Sherlock, honestly, a dragon? They only exist in storybooks."

"Not necessarily," exclaims the voice again.

Irene begins to make her way out of the laboratory. Holmes is not pleased with her and isn't moving to see her out. "If I just have a day or two," he mutters, "then so be it. Lestrade may not be giving me even that."

"Well, Saint George, let me know when you slay your dragon."

Laughter erupts upstairs.

Irene stops and sighs. She looks sympathetically at Sherlock. "Though I know this search will lead you nowhere, if I were you, and I wanted more information about Hemsworth, the *real* goods, I'd start with one Mr. Hilton Poke. He knows everyone's secrets. I am sure His Highness has some, but as I think you will see, not enough to make him a murderer. Speak to Poke – it might help you consider better suspects."

She clatters from the lab and into the outer room. The entrance opens and closes and as it does, the apothecary flies down the spiral staircase and rushes past the boy and out of doors. He is holding a piece of paper and an ink bottle. Moments pass, then he returns. He hands the paper to Sherlock.

"What is this?"

"A note to Mr. Poke from Irene Doyle, introducing you. He is a man who is impressed by, shall we say, position. You and I, boy, we have none. Mr. Andrew C. Doyle has much more. Poke will see you if you bear this note. You shall be turned away without it."

Sherlock Holmes is well aware of Hilton Poke, the gossip
columnist for *The News of the World*, who is said to know
everything about every theatrical star in London, or at least
everything that they don't want the public to know. Much to
his shame, Holmes reads the little man's stories regularly.

The newspaper's offices are on Fleet Street, a busy
avenue in the very center of London where most publica-
tions are headquartered. Sherlock has no other leads, so he
heads there early the next morning, out into a day that is
already humid. He picks his way through the noisy crowds,
past the four-storey buildings that line both sides of the
curving street that runs uphill from Trafalgar Square to
St. Paul's Cathedral. He keeps his eye out for blue-coated
members of the Force, who might be coming his way with
orders to take him to Scotland Yard. But none approach.
Halfway down Fleet, he spots the red canopy with the globe
and the newspaper's name. When he tells the lady at the
front counter that he has important information for Hilton
Poke, he is directed up a staircase and down a hot hallway.
The columnist has one of the largest offices in the building,
with a good view of Fleet Street. Its mahogany walls are
plastered with photographs, drawings, and caricatures of the
city's current theatrical stars. Poke is sitting in his chair with
his feet up on his desk, waving a peacock-feather fan in his
face. Despite that, the sweat still pours down his forehead
and soaks through his white shirt and dark brown suitcoat.
His countenance is that of a weasel, his body the build of a
beaver. His lispy voice, which he is forever attempting to
lower, rises up and down like the waves on the English

Channel, and everything he says is spoken as though it were of the gravest importance. His darting eyes rarely meet others', and they certainly don't now, as he takes Irene Doyle's note from the poorly dressed boy. He reads it.

"Hmmph! Her father was once a name in this town – I suppose he helped a few folks – but he is fast descending. I hear Miss Doyle wants to sing, silly girl. His Highness Hemsworth? Why should I speak with you about him?"

"Because I know things."

Poke studies the boy.

"What do you know?"

Sherlock hesitates. "Venus, his assistant, does not . . ."

"It is old news to me that she is actually from Brixton. I am waiting for the best moment to reveal that tasty tidbit. Not yet, not a big enough bang available presently."

Sherlock had not intended to reveal that morsel about Juliet. He had planned a more meager revelation – merely that Venus wears English-style dresses offstage. "But you can't tell the public that," says Sherlock. "That would ruin her, take her job from her!"

Poke gives him a withering look. "Anything else?"

Sherlock tries a few other scraps of information he has picked up over the last week, nothing to do with the crime, nothing about the inner chamber. But what he offers is obviously old news to the gossip columnist, or at least of insufficient sensation. Poke takes a few seconds to stare back blankly, as if he were a king and the boy a pauper, then looks away again. So . . . Holmes plays his ace.

"I have friends at Scotland Yard."

"You?"

"I am close to Inspector Lestrade's son."

"Yes?"

"He has given me some inside information, and, using it, we have made some progress on the Nottingham murder. The public knows nothing of it. This is between you and me."

Poke leans forward. "What information?"

"I can't tell you."

The fat little man swings his feet off the desk and stands up. "Then you can see yourself out." He turns to examine his bookcase, as if he has much more important things to do. There are just four or five books on the entire shelf, all biographies of show-business stars, two by Hilton Poke himself.

Sherlock stays seated. "I believe we can get Hemsworth convicted of the crime."

Poke glances around at the boy. "Go on."

"If you are willing to tell me all you know about him, it will help us immensely."

"My dear boy, I need one of two people to be found guilty of this murder. If you cross your heart and swear to die that you have a reasonable chance to bring either His Highness Hemsworth . . . or the deliciously intriguing Mrs. Nottingham before the magistrates, then I shall help you. I could care less who really did it. But either of those two in the dock would work well for my purposes. Either would be a sensation!"

Sherlock reluctantly crosses his heart and hopes to die, something he hasn't done since he was a small child. "Tell me what you know, Mr. Poke, and I will do what I can. I am guessing the police have not spoken to you . . . they would not understand the depths of your knowledge of the things that really matter."

Poke commences to spill the beans. Most of it is useless gossip and childish rumors about Hemsworth's private life – sensational stories about the time he was captured in the Far East and brutally tattooed while tied by all four limbs to the ground; tales of the three-headed creatures and talking baboons he found on his travels; the "fact" that when he finishes with the small animals in his acts he guillotines them for amusement; that Venus will soon bear his child; several stories of his taste for drinking blood, and the twice-verified rumor that he was bitten by a vampire. Poke is obviously trying too hard, working at coming up with any morsel he has been fed that might make Hemsworth look like a killer. Sherlock is disappointed. It is all nonsense. But one thing intrigues him. There is a recurring theme in the columnist's information.

"Might I stop you there for a moment, sir?"

"Intriguing, isn't it? Too much to take in at once?"

"You keep mentioning that there is evidence that he is a vampire. That, in itself, does not interest me. It is non-sense. Vampires are figments of the human imagination, arising from our inner fears, placed in stories to thrill and scare people who have no brains in their heads."

"Look, boy, if –"

"But . . ."

"But what?"

"Tell me why your sources believe he is one. It keeps coming up in what you say."

"Well . . . the most telling thing is that he hates the sunlight."

"Hates it?"

"He is nocturnal, my dear. I have heard that from many of my people."

"But I saw him rehearsing in the theater one day. And he performs in the evenings under very bright stage lights."

"That is not sunlight, you nincompoop. He is rarely seen outside during the day, but he is up all night, every night. We have spotted him on many occasions in the small hours of the morning."

Sherlock's eyes grow wide. "Thank you, Mr. Poke," he says, springing to his feet and shaking the gossip columnist's sweaty little hand.

"But I haven't told you everything that –"

Holmes is already out the door and rushing down the hallway.

Hemsworth is rarely seen during the day. The boy has an idea.

16

HIS VAMPIRE WAYS

Sherlock can hardly wait until the sun sets. He stays out of sight in the shop, never once peeking his head out the door for the rest of the morning or the entire afternoon, contenting himself with his chores, anxious every time there is a knock at the entrance. Then, telling no one, not the police, young Lestrade, Irene, or even Sigerson Bell, he makes his way to The Egyptian Hall. Curiously, he doesn't leave on time to arrive for the performance. He goes out about half an hour before it ends, while there is still sunlight, and doesn't stop near the marquee on Piccadilly Street. Instead, he slips down the alley at the side and waits in the growing darkness at the rear. Almost immediately, he hears the audience leaving at the front of the building, then Venus comes out, glances around, and rushes away. Things quiet down, the crowd disperses, and finally, Hemsworth appears, his expression grim, as it always seems to be when he is alone. He heads up the alley and into his hansom cab on Piccadilly.

Sherlock doesn't budge. He stays in the shadows, which soon cover the alley and the entire little courtyard at the rear of the theater. Buildings loom on all sides. Darkness descends on London. There are no gaslights here and it grows pitch black. He presses his left arm against his side and feels the horsewhip's hard, leather surface under his sleeve. He is nervous, and not just because of the lack of light or what he plans to do tonight. His jumpiness has been with him since he left Denmark Street.

Someone is following him, again.

He is absolutely sure now. *Is it Riyah?* Possibly. *Could it be Malefactor?* He doubts that. But it might be Crew. Whoever it is, he is large, adult size. This would be bad news under any circumstances, but it is especially disconcerting tonight, during this dangerous, post-midnight mission. He slides down against the brick wall of the building adjacent to The Egyptian Hall and tries not to fall asleep. He wishes he could keep surveying the area, as he did when he first arrived. But the moonlight is meager tonight: he can barely see more than a few feet in front of his face. And he keeps hearing things. There is that constant jingle and clap of horses and carriages and other city sounds in the distance, but back here in the dark, there are noises too – the shuffling of feet, it seems, the creaking of boards, and footsteps. He tries to remain still. The hours pass. He hears Big Ben to the south-east at the Parliament Buildings, gonging midnight, then one o'clock, two, and then three.

Then it happens . . . just as he suspected.

A light appears at the other end of the courtyard, in the back alley that leads the other way: out of this tight space and away from the theater, running under a high catwalk between two buildings into narrow Jermyn Street.

The artery is barely wide enough for a carriage. Accompanying the light is the sound of four horses' hooves on the cobblestones, and behind them, now coming dimly into view, a long coach, unique in appearance, built low to the ground like a big casket. Its driver negotiates a little circle in the tight courtyard, bringing his vehicle up to the wide, stablelike door at the back of the theater. A man jumps down from the seat, carrying a bull's eye lantern. It is the vampire himself . . . Alistair Hemsworth!

He unlocks the theater's wide back door and slides it open. It is elevated about a carriage wheel's height above the ground, perfect, when fitted with a ramp, for deliveries or horses moving in and out.

A piece of brick falls from somewhere. It narrowly misses Sherlock. Hemsworth turns and surveys the courtyard. His light almost spots the boy.

"Just rats," says someone sitting in the passenger seat in the driver's box. Holmes hadn't noticed him before. The boy squints in the darkness and sees the dim profile of a black felt hat, long black hair, and what looks like a greatcoat over the man's shoulders. Hemsworth jumps up into the stable-door threshold and enters the rear of The Egyptian Hall. In seconds, he is pulling a ramp out from the building and into the back of the coach. He sets it up so he has a bridge. He goes back into the Hall once more and doesn't come out again for ten minutes or so. Then strange sounds come from just inside the theater – heavy breathing, shuffling feet, and a clanking noise. The vehicle's passenger gets out and stands facing the commotion – pointing a rifle in its direction. Hemsworth reappears, moving backwards, the lantern around his shoulders, quietly cooing at something he has on a chain. It's held back by a long pole he has fastened to its neck. It is four-legged, something like eight feet long, its head about three feet high. His Highness is cautious with it – it's obviously stronger than he is – and it seems to be shackled at the legs. The boy can't see it clearly, but it appears to be muzzled, too. The other man still has the gun trained on it. The magician bends down and goes into the low vehicle with the creature, keeping more than an arm's length ahead. When they have disappeared, there is the sound of clanging irons, then Hemsworth pops out of the front of the coach, slams down a door to seal the back from the driver's box and gets into his seat. The other man lowers his rifle, fastens the coach's rear door, closes up the building, and moves around to the passenger side. He stops for a moment, and looks at the courtyard and alley again while Hemsworth flashes his light about. Then the passenger crawls up into his seat. Hemsworth snaps the whip, and the horses shoot out the back alley, under the catwalk, and into Jermyn Street.

Sherlock swings into action, racing from his hiding spot and chasing the vehicle. It turns right at the street. *It is going west . . . in the direction of the Cremorne Gardens.* But suddenly, he hears someone shout.

"Stop!"

The boy freezes. The voice is familiar, though deeper than he remembers.

"Who is there?"

For a moment, there is silence. Then, that voice again.

"Sherlock Holmes, I perceive."

He is on the roof. He doesn't show himself, but there is no doubt who it is.

Malefactor.

"You have returned?"

"I have never been away."

Sherlock looks up and sees a shadowy figure in a top hat and tailcoat, twirling a walking stick.

"Well, that is lovely to know, and I would be thrilled to hear all your news, but I'm rather busy right now."

"No, you're not."

"I'm not?"

"You shall not be pursuing this case. It is of interest to *me*. If he really has a dragon, then I want it. I can use it. A dragon is gold, and believe me, we all want gold . . . even you, Holmes, though you'd never admit it."

"Stay out of this."

"Funny you say that, I was just about to add those very words."

"I won't –"

"Don't challenge me, Jew-boy. You never should have before. That was a big mistake. And now, my powers have grown."

"Odors increased too, I assume?"

"Yes, you do always assume. You have assumed too much in *this* case, for example. Freed Hemsworth, did we? Tut-tut."

"Go away, Malefactor, or I will make you disappear for good. Remember, I have the law on my side. What do you have? You work alone now, I see."

"Oh, believe me, I am not alone. And never shall be. In fact, my web has spun wider and will keep growing. I am getting my education, will make myself into a learned man some day, little one, a scholar with a spotless record even you will not be able to question, someone even Miss Doyle could admire. You shall see. Mathematics is my subject, of course – chaos theory: I think I have it down now. It's most helpful in my line of business. But despite all of that, from here onward, I will do my best work in the shadows."

"Show yourself!"

"Never!"

"Coward!"

"Well, maybe just a little."

The figure emerges toward the edge of the rooftop. It pulls a lantern out from behind its back and holds it under its chin, lighting the face in a lurid way. Even from a distance, Sherlock can see the bulging forehead, the sunken eyes, the darting lizard-like tongue, and above it a developing mustache. He looks even taller, a little older.

"I was forced to take some odd jobs lately, due to you . . . but as I say, I will soon be a respectable man, a fake like everyone of that ilk. I shall pop up soon in that guise, hidden in plain view. You know what they say . . . Satan is often a Man of Peace. It is all plotted, the future is set. I hear *you* still assist a poor apothecary."

"It is a passing occupation."

"Don't disown or deny the ones you care for, Holmes."

"I would love to chat, but I must be going."

Sherlock turns to run through the little courtyard and out the alleyway to Jermyn Street. The coach is well on its way. He will have to sprint to catch it, and to lose Malefactor at the same time.

"Gentlemen!" shouts his rival.

Immediately, two figures emerge at the Jermyn Street end of the alley, under the catwalk, facing Sherlock, and coming toward him: a small one to the left, a large one to the right. *Grimsby and Crew.* He can't see their faces, but he imagines the little one's ghoulish grin and the big one's blank stare.

Sherlock stops in his tracks. He can't go this direction. But if he turns and runs the other way, back out the alley behind him, he will have no chance to catch Hemsworth's vehicle. He feels for his horsewhip, then looks toward the two thugs and decides.

He turns around and runs, right under Malefactor, up the alleyway and out into Piccadilly. It is time to cut his losses. *There is no advantage to being caught.* Those two henchmen could put him out of commission for a long while. He reaches the street and keeps running, all the way to the apothecary shop.

But he doesn't stay there. In fact, he doesn't even venture past the front room and into the laboratory. He merely slips inside, stays long enough for anyone who might be following him to assume that he will not reemerge, and goes out again. Bell doesn't seem to be present.

Then, Sherlock takes a strange route to the Cremorne Gardens, sticking to alleys, mews, and small streets. It isn't the safest way, but it's the smartest, calculated to make pursuit a difficult endeavor. He sees many street people, stable boys, and thugs, and rushes by lowlifes who are making decisions about how to rob him. He is trying to move as quickly as he can, but stares right back when they look at him, as he once watched Malefactor teach his minions to do – *show no fear, let them know that there are better, less resistant targets* – and scurries onward.

When he gets to Chelsea, he can see that no vehicle has entered through the Cremorne gates off King's Road – it is locked tight and there are no discernable wheel tracks. So, rather than crossing through the Gardens to the back of the hotel, as he has before, he heads down the street that runs along the east end of the park, until he is almost at the river. There he turns and walks to the front of The World's End. Everything looks quiet. He spies a couple of policemen who think they are perfectly disguised as street people, and avoids them. There is a stable door near the front entrance, but given this police presence, Hemsworth would not have tried to unload his freight here. *Or would he? What magic is he capable of?* There is one more Gardens' gate, on the south side at the river past the west end of the hotel, but when Sherlock gets there, it too, is locked and the ground undisturbed. Of course, there is another possibility. *He hasn't come here at all.*

Sherlock makes sure the plainclothes policemen aren't near, jumps the fence, and enters the Gardens. *Where is Scuttle? He would be helpful now.*

The boy arrives almost on cue, as he does every time, it seems. He is again anxious to be seen and listened to, despite it being almost five o'clock in the morning. He is wearing his usual clothes, or lack of them, and doesn't appear to have been recently asleep. Sherlock motions for him to move a good distance away from the hotel, out into the Gardens.

"Under the covers again, sir? I am at your servicement once more."

"Good."

"Good?" the little boy swallows. "You knows, sir, there are many policemen wearing very plain clothing tonight. We must not do anything too conspicuating."

"Let me ask you a question, Scuttle."

"I am a seasoning answerer, my excellent man. I have answered many questions over my years, I 'ave. I answered the queen, you knows. Did I tell you?"

"Yes, you did."

"And I answered those who 'ave starred at the Theatre Royal in Drury Lane, no less, and the Garrick and the 'aymarket, all the best 'alls. I answered Sayers the boxing man and Leybourne who sings of the flying young man on the daring trapeze, and Mr. Lear who makes up nonsense, and each and every one of the Davenport Brothers, they who disappear on the stages. Without a doubt . . . I've answered all the important people in the empire."

"Then answer this. Does Hemsworth have a real dragon?"

"Oh, no doubt, sir, no doubt."

"Can you prove it?"

"Well . . . well . . ."

"I need to prove it."

"It is within the mighty realms of possibility that I may 'ave spoken too dramatically just now, too not realistically. 'e may not have a dragon, sir. I have never seen 'im with one, sir, now that I thinks of it."

"Then what *does* he have? You have seen him sneaking around the park. Does he keep something down there?"

"Down where?"

"In his inner room, his second chamber?"

"Second chamber, sir? I 'ave been in there, and there is only one."

Have been in there? There is only one?

"Let me stop you there, my good man. You have said two things that intrigue me."

"That does not surprise me, sir. Even The Prince of the Whales was intrigued by Scuttle's talk, 'e who makes foreign affairs with beautiful ladies who are married to other fine gentlemen, which England accepts, understanding 'is importance, and loving to 'ear of his romantics, as they are time-consummating and of fascination."

"Scuttle! *Listen* to me. This is important."

"I shall become full of ears, and yet –"

"Shut your face, sir, until I am done."

There is silence.

"Scuttle, what do you mean when you say you have been in there? How is that possible?"

There is more silence.

"You can talk now. Answer the question please, but stick to the subject."

"I . . . 'ave . . . been . . . inside . . . Mr. 'emsworth's studio."

"When?"

"Many times."

"Many times? Why?"

"The keeper, Mr. Starr, 'e asks Scuttle to water the tropical plants and mooshrooms in that room, as Mr. 'emsworth is away from times to times. They is vampire plants, foreign ones from fars away – they need no sun, just like 'im. I does it during the days when there is no one about. I am told not to touch anything. And I doesn't . . . 'cept I looks at the magic tricks . . . a little. I was told to keep what I does quiet, so I never even whispered of it to the police, or to you, my agent. I do as I'm told when on wery important duties. Just told the Inspector, when 'e asked, that I thought the place was Mr. 'emsworth's, because I felt it was 'im I seen goings in and goings out on many occasions . . . just as I often see, and speak to the great and famous Mrs. Keene, the important and stunned actress who –"

"Scuttle, let's stay on our subject, remember?"

"Yes, sir, I shall stick like 'orse glue to our subject on which we are gabbing."

"Have you been in there lately, since the police have been guarding it so closely?"

"Yes, sir, there is great need for the watering of plants now, as the magical magician 'isself is not allowed in neither."

"How closely do the police watch you?"

"They stops me every time, sir, to make sure it is Scuttle."

That means I can't go disguised as this boy.

"The second thing you said of interest was that you

thought there was only one room down there. But there is a second one . . . behind a wall. In fact, there are three."

The smaller boy pauses. "Sir, are you right in your upper storeys? That sounds like a wery fantastic idea from a novel for a child or a panting-mime on the London stage. But 'ere, sir, under the 'otel, there is just one large room."

"No, Scuttle, there are three. And in the third room, he may be keeping something."

The smaller boy swallows again. "Something?"

"Something living; a beast of some sort, I think. I don't know what it is, but I heard noises."

Scuttle steps back.

Sherlock speaks softly "I have a secret assignment for you. I will give you several tuppence to do it. This is *very* secret, even the plainclothes policemen are not aware of it, and must not be told."

"Yes?"

"And I cannot go myself, so I will entrust this to you."

"Yes?"

"Could you go inside tonight, saying that you need to water the plants?"

"And what . . . what would I do then?"

"Go into the second chamber. I will tell you how. Then, proceed down into the third, and report back to me tomorrow on what you see."

Scuttle is silent.

"Master Scuttle?"

"Is this for England, sir?"

"Yes. Yes, it is."

"But what if Scuttle is wery nervewacking, sir? What if my 'eart sweats and my 'ands pound, and my brain shakes so as I cannot do the duty?"

"Just imagine you are onstage. . . . Imagine you are the star in a very important play."

"A famous one? Perhaps one that might cause a scandal due to its racing subject? Perhaps Scuttle could be wery dashing and 'andsome in it?"

"Yes, something like that."

"I will do it . . . and become famous in real life too for 'elping to solve this murder."

"Uh, that may not happen. Remember, this is a secret mission. You are doing this because it is the right thing to do – for justice."

"But that is not a good reason to do something, sir, just ask anyone in our modern world."

"Then . . . *pretend*, Scuttle."

"Ah!"

"You will do it?"

"I awaits your commandment."

"You must go now."

"Now?"

"Time is of the essence."

Scuttle doesn't move. "There is nervousment inside me, sir, great nervousment."

"Just pretend, Scuttle, remember? *Pretend.*"

The little boy squints his eyes and imagines. When he opens them, he looks calmer. Sherlock tells him how to get into the second chamber, and then watches him march off. He sees him stop next to a plainclothes policeman, then head toward the back door of the hotel with the key he's been given. Poor Scuttle disappears inside.

THE INNER CHAMBER

After just a few hours of sleep, Sherlock is back on his feet, hoping that Lestrade is not coming for him. He prays he can just have this day, and more importantly, this night. There is no sign of the police in or near the apothecary shop. Bell sits at the laboratory table eating more of those scones with tea. His eyes dart up as the boy seizes a scone to eat, another to shove in a pocket, and pours a hot flask of tea down his throat.

"Sir, why are you not speaking to me?"

"I do not see you there. I do not see that you will not be doing your shop chores, tending to the store, or practicing your lessons with me today."

"But –"

"Go! Go . . . before I notice you and make you stay."

Sherlock rushes toward the door, but can't resist asking Bell one question before heading out into the streets.

"Do you really think Hemsworth has a dragon, sir?"

"There is more in this world, Master Holmes, than is dreamt of in your imagination . . . and, by the way, if you see said Holmes, tell him he has work to do today and must come home immediately!"

But Sherlock doesn't get all the way down Denmark Street. He is accosted just before it meets Crown Street.

"Oh, thank goodness, you are all right."

"Uh . . . of course, I am, Miss Leckie."

"A friend of mine, a younger one who is going to the summer classes at Snowfields, told me you were not there yesterday, and I met 'er on my way in, just an 'alf hour ago, near the school, and I 'ad 'er run in to see if you were attending today. She said you were nowhere to be seen. I came right 'ere."

Her eyes are red.

"I have a few approved days away. You must be late for your work."

"I shall make up the time. I just wanted to be sure you weren't 'urt, or worse. I remembered 'ow anxious you still were about this Nottingham case the last time we spoke . . . you were fussing about it, but not telling me exactly why . . . and I recollected the time you went back to that awful 'otel where the murder 'appened . . . and I was worried you 'ad done something like that again."

"As you see, I am as fit as a fiddle."

She puts a hand on his arm. "Don't let Miss Doyle lead you into doing more dangerous things. I am sure she is a wonderful lady, and I know she is so pretty and all, but be careful, Sherlock."

Would Irene ever be like this?

"Miss Doyle is actually encouraging me to stay out of the Nottingham investigation."

"She is? Well . . . she is right, then. She has changed 'er mind?"

"She got what she wanted when Hemsworth was freed."

"But you . . . you aren't done with this, are you?"

"Not exactly."

"What does that mean?"

"Beatrice . . . I really think Hemsworth may have done it." *Why am I telling her this? Do girls just get whatever they want from me?*

"So . . . is this why you aren't at school?"

She knows, of course. "Yes."

The boy doesn't like standing still. He looks behind, up at the rooftops. *No sign of Malefactor or his henchmen, no police, but I must get moving.*

"Are you going somewhere now about this case?"

"I'm just . . . dropping by the market for Mr. Bell."

"No, you're not."

I swear they are mind readers.

"You are right, I'm not. But I must be off."

"Back to The World's End?"

Sherlock begins to walk slowly. Beatrice strolls with him, taking his arm. But as they turn south on Crown Street, he sees a small, black-coated figure dart into an alleyway no more than fifty yards ahead, on their side of the street. *Grimsby.* Beatrice feels Sherlock stiffen.

"I am being followed."

"Fifty yards ahead, our side, alley."

"How . . . how did you know that?"

"I am poor, Sherlock, and a girl, so I know when I am being followed or watched, believe me. Your upbringing in our neighborhood 'elps you to know when you are in danger, but if you were a girl, that sense would be even better."

He had never thought of it like that.

"Keep walking," she adds.

"What?"

"Let's just walk right past 'im."

They cross in front of the alley.

"I wish you weren't doing dangerous things, but it is what you want to do, what you *need* to do, because of your mother and something inside you. So, you should do it." She pauses. "When I say *now*, run. Be careful, Sherlock. . . . Now!"

Grimsby has left the alley and filed into the crowd on the foot pavement no more than ten feet behind them. Beatrice turns, walks directly at him, takes his arm and pivots him so he points in the opposite direction. He tries to wrench himself from her, violently pulling back his arm.

"Oh, you vile beast!" shouts Beatrice. A group of gentlemen quickly surround Grimsby, each one angrily asking him if this is how he treats a lady. They won't let him go. Sherlock runs. In seconds, Grimsby has been lost.

Holmes tries not to think of what Beatrice did for him as he moves briskly south and west through London to Chelsea. *Concentrate.* The gates are not open yet at the Cremorne Gardens, and he has to be very careful getting over the wrought-iron fence in broad daylight, but he succeeds and goes in search of Scuttle. He can hardly wait to hear what he discovered. But an hour later, Sherlock still can't find him. He looks everywhere and then begins to panic. The little boy's broken dustbin, where he sleeps, is empty.

The Cremorne opens for the day – the music fills the park, dancers gather in the pagodas, hawkers cry their ices and cold refreshments, stilt-walkers move about the crowds, and the circus performers get ready. But still, no Scuttle. Sherlock leaves the Gardens and heads around its exterior to the front entrance of the hotel. He knows this isn't smart during the day, but he must locate the boy.

"You!" someone shouts.

Harrison Starr is pointing a finger at him and coming his way. Normally, Holmes would run, but he wants to know about his little friend.

"Sir, have you seen . . ."

"I will do the talking. I am being generous as it is, allowing you to even be here. We have an emergency this morning. Young Scuttle is missing."

Sherlock's heart leaps.

"I . . ."

"Have you seen him?"

". . . no."

"If you do, alert the authorities at once. Scuttle is always out and about in the mornings, always speaks to me at exactly 8 a.m. at the back entrance, so it is very disturbing that he did not appear and can't be found. The police are suspecting foul play. . . . It is a terrible thing . . . poor little boy; he was such a fine lad. We are all half expecting his body to turn up soon." Starr walks away, so preoccupied that he doesn't even send Holmes off the grounds.

But the boy is barely able to move, anyway. *First, I nearly had Irene killed during the Whitechapel case, then . . . then my mother . . . I even put Mr. Bell in danger . . . then Beatrice takes Grimsby's very arm to help me . . . and now, Scuttle, that little chap who wouldn't hurt a flea . . . who didn't want to go down there.*

"Sherlock!"

He nearly jumps out of his skin.

"I didn't mean to startle you." It's young Lestrade, who has an irritating ability to sneak up on others. "But I thought I should warn you. Father hasn't heard anything from you and he is very impatient about this case. You must produce something he can use now . . . or he will ruin you. He said this morning that he wants you found. They sent someone to Denmark Street about half of an hour ago."

"Thank you," says Sherlock and slouches away. He heads for the river, one of his black moods descending on him.

The shoreline of the Thames varies a great deal as it winds through London. In some places there are piers, wharves, or docks jutting out into the water, in other spots there are buildings set right to the edge – factories and warehouses on the south side, more attractive structures on the north – but other areas have rough beaches of pebbles or mud, stretching down to the brown-gray water. The Thames's thirteen bridges are all different too. As Sherlock trudges away from the Gardens down to the shore, he sees one of the most westerly viaducts, the Battersea, to his left. One of the oldest bridges on the river, the only one made out of wood, it looks rickety and medieval compared to the stone and cast-iron crossings in the center of the city. Those bridges are always packed with surging crowds and buzzing with noise, while Battersea has few pedestrians or carriages moving across its narrow gravel surface. Boats of all sizes jam the river to the east, toward Westminster. But from where he stands to the bridge, a distance of some several hundred yards, few people frequent the shoreline. He hears the gulls and just the odd human voice crying out in the morning mist. Below Cremorne Road, which runs along the edge of the bank, he sees the people called mudlarks searching for things washed up on the beach, paupers wandering about, and scrawny, barely clothed children with bare feet, trying to play. Other bodies lie still, faces ghostly white, fast asleep on the wet ground. The day is gray. There is no wonder they call this part of Chelsea, The World's End. Sherlock looks toward Battersea Bridge again and notices a ramp leading down from Beaufort Street onto the beach. He wonders if he should cross into Battersea, head south. *Where should I go?* Whatever he does, he cannot be near the Gardens, the hotel, his father, or the apothecary shop.

Perhaps he should find Beatrice . . . or make his way to Bloomsbury and Irene. Instead, feeling sorry for himself, he walks aimlessly. He takes the stone steps down from Cremorne Road onto the stretch of mud near the water. A voice cries out from up above and he instinctively ducks, covering his face. But when he glances up to the road, no one is looking down. He knows the Force *will* look, even here, very soon.

Holmes takes off his frock coat and turns it inside out, making it appear tattered. He pulls the collar up. He takes off his boots and stuffs them inside the coat, and buttons it around them, creating a big belly for himself. He rolls his trouser legs up to his knees, then smears mud on his face and runs it through his hair. And when he begins to walk again, he bends over, making himself look shorter. It isn't his best disguise, but hopefully it will work. If the police look for him here, they likely won't come down to the water, just search from above, instead. They won't view him up close. He hopes Lestrade isn't really after him anyway. *They want me out of their hair, away from the crime scene and the theater. But if I can't go to either of those places . . . then what can I do?*

He walks slowly along the shore. *It, indeed, feels like the end of the world here.* All the action is up above at the Gardens, or to the north and the east; there is even much more activity, of a working-class sort, to the south toward Battersea Park and the factories. It occurs to him that someone could wander this area for a long time, down near the water in this sparser part of western London, and virtually no one would –

No one would notice you!

Sherlock halts suddenly and stops thinking about himself. Something else has entered his thoughts. *Hemsworth and the secret contents of his strange vehicle . . . going west.* He looks downriver to the ancient wooden bridge, remembering the little ramp he has just seen there. He walks toward it, the moist sand poking up between his toes. *What is it?* It becomes clearer. *A little road that leads down to the beach!* He has never observed such a thing at other bridges. Usually, it is almost impossible to take a carriage or a wagon of any sort down near the Thames. However . . . if you wanted to do it here, and approach the Cremorne Gardens unseen, you could do it via that ramp and this shoreline, away from the population, moving past drunks and paupers and children and mudlarks at night. *But where, exactly, could you go?* Sherlock turns around and heads back to the Gardens at a hurried pace, trusting that his disguise and his distance from the upper roads will keep him unrecognized. It occurs to him, as he moves, that not only is the Gardens directly above the high bank at the river . . . The World's End Hotel is right there too.

Growing more excited, his black mood instantly gone, he approaches the Gardens, though he walks on an angle, away from the banks and out to the river, until his bare feet are in the water. From here, he can see up above the banks. *The hotel is, indeed, right there.* He can see the top of its black roof and one of its gothic turrets. The big building virtually hangs out over the river. Unable to stay calm, he sprints toward the bank. He slows as he nears, and examines the surface of the shoreline beneath his feet, observing faint remnants of wheel tracks close to the banks, coming from the direction of the bridge. They are difficult to make out, having been washed over by the tide, but he can judge where they are headed.

As he approaches the bank, he realizes that there is absolutely no one on the shoreline right there. He glances around. No one is looking his way from a distance either, from up above or down below. At the bank, he spots footprints in the sand in front of bushes. There is something unusual about these shrubs. He doesn't have to tug hard on the branches to pull everything away. *They aren't rooted.* In fact, they are, upon close examination . . . stage foliage, just like the jungle trees in Hemsworth's act. Hands shaking, he separates them and sees an opening in the steep bank behind them, not much more than four feet wide and six feet high. He strides through the bushes and carefully puts them back into place behind him.

There is a tunnel in front of him. *What did Riyah tell him about the inner chamber? He said there were stories that it was once a dungeon, used by William the Conqueror during the 11ᵗʰ century. Were victims brought in this way, up or down the river, and then secreted into a dungeon?* It is very narrow and low. *But Hemsworth's strangely shaped vehicle had about the same dimensions!*

Within a few yards, Sherlock encounters a door. Thick and made of iron, fitted tightly into the rock, it is obviously meant to keep out curious trespassers who may get past the façade of bushes. It is locked shut.

The boy takes off his frock coat, turns it back the way it should be and puts it on again, then pulls his boots on too. He may need to be able to move quickly. Though he has his horsewhip with him, he didn't think it necessary to bring a knife when he left the shop this morning. But he does have a way to open this lock, not the best means, but hopefully it will do. He reaches into a pocket to find the little wire he has carried with him every day for more than two years, since he helped solve the case of the Whitechapel murder: the wire his rival unwittingly taught him how to use. *Malefactor.* He steps back out toward the beach and looks along the river in both directions. *No one watching.* At least, no one he can see. He returns to the door, sticks the little wire into it, and in minutes has it unlatched.

What will be inside?

His heart pounding, he slowly opens the door, steps through, and leaves it very slightly ajar. *I can't lock myself in.* It is pitch black inside. He has just one Lucifer and a small candle left in his pocket. He strikes the match and lights it. *Will this light last long enough to get me to wherever this leads? . . . Will it still be burning on the way out?*

He walks slowly. The passage is barely taller than his head and continues to be just a little more than four feet across. *People were smaller in those days. Hemsworth's vehicle would just fit in here, as tight as an arm in a sleeve. It must be a ghastly trip*, he thinks, *going through here in the dark with that beast, or whatever it is.*

Sherlock hears very little at first, just the sound of water dripping and the echo of his footsteps on the rock floor. But as he moves forward, he begins to hear other noises, somewhere farther along the tunnel. As he gets closer, it becomes clear that they are screams . . . and they sound human.

DEATH IN THE CHAMBER

Sherlock begins to run along the dim tunnel. But about a hundred paces in, he realizes he has made a big mistake: the passageway is not as dark here, which indicates that he is moving toward lights; it also means that whoever or whatever is up ahead – a villain, or a murderous beast of some sort – he, she, or it, will soon see *his* light. *I must approach in total darkness.* He slows. *I need to douse the candle.* But if he does, he will have no light to find his way out. If this tunnel leads to the lower chamber, he will not be able to leave through the hotel basement either, because the exits are guarded by the police. His only way out is via the door he came in. *Should I go back while I have a light? Get out while I can?* But he knows that if he goes now, without any evidence, he won't be able to convince the police to come here and investigate, no matter how much he pleads. They will simply accost him the moment they spot him. Lestrade won't listen to him. The only solution to this entire mess is to find the dragon, or its equivalent; to find Nottingham's murderer. *And I cannot just turn away from whoever is in peril. I must go in there, toward those screams.*

Holmes puts out the candle.

As he gets closer to the lighted area, the screams grow in volume. It sounds like someone, or something, is in pain. It is as if he or she or it is being tortured. But the screams are not all he hears. They are interspersed with barks, but they don't sound like they are coming from a dog.

He stops about fifty feet from the light. From this vantage point he cannot see anything in the dimly lit chamber except the stone wall at its far end, and a torch hanging from it. But there are shadows moving about. He hears those barks again, screams, and now squeals. Amidst it all, he thinks he hears a human moan. He moves a little closer.

Then he sees something.

A figure moves past, going from right to left in the chamber. Sherlock flattens himself against the wall, and then cautiously looks toward it. It is nearly five feet tall . . . and not human. It seems to be doing the barking, though it *definitely* isn't a dog. It ambles on four legs but then stops and stands up on two, looking around as if sensing an intruder. Sherlock pulls his head back. It has something in its hands, which is struggling, screaming, trying to get away. The boy peers out again. The smaller, writhing creature is a small monkey. The big one that grips it – brown and furry – lowers its head and bites it; and it stops screaming and gasps. Then the larger creature continues on its way across the room to Holmes' left and disappears down a ramp into what seems to be a pit. Sherlock hears a horrible hissing sound and the little monkey screams again; there is a great thrashing about and gnashing of teeth . . . the noise of a huge animal gobbling up another. Then the big creature appears again. Sherlock can see it clearly now, face-on: a frightening canine-like visage, with a muzzle and close-set black eyes, framed by sand-colored hair . . . an immense, dog-faced ape.

A baboon!

Sherlock has read about them in journals. They are found in Africa and areas of Asia. He thinks there may be a few at the Zoological Society's Gardens in Regent's Park. This one seems enormous, as if someone has fed it too much and altered it somehow. The boy recalls what he knows of them. They are aggressive, the males (which this one obviously is) have teeth the size of human thumbs, and they are omnivorous, eating not just fruit and vegetation . . . but other animals too.

Sherlock lets his horsewhip slide down in his sleeve.

Then he hears that moan . . . the human moan. He freezes, and as he does, the baboon passes by again, this time going back to his right. Then there is the sound of a cage rattling, a latch being opened, an ear-splitting squeal, and the ape appears once more, now with a big rat in his hand. It ambles across the space and heads toward the pit. Sherlock steps into the room from behind, carefully watching the back of the baboon's head as it descends to the place where the horrific sounds came from just moments ago.

It is feeding live animals to something.

The boy turns to examine the room and what he sees shocks him. Directly before him, against the wall and to his right, is a row of cages in which rats, monkeys, and pigs are held. They stare out at him in fear, squealing and chattering. The last cage, in the corner, is twice as large as the others –

obviously intended for bigger creatures. *What else, in God's name, has been fed to that beast?* Then he glimpses a large animal of some sort lying on the wet stone inside that cage, barely noticeable in the far corner. It looks weak and is moaning. Sherlock realizes that it is a human being . . . a small one . . . *Scuttle!*

The cage latches are simple ones, opened with keys, hanging from poles just a few feet away from each prison, just beyond the reach of the captives. *The baboon must have been taught to open each cage, take out an animal, lock it again, and put up the key.* Sherlock hears the hissing again from the pit, the thrashing sounds, the rat squealing, and the crunching of small bones. Then he sees the baboon's head rising up above the ramp on its way back, to retrieve more live food for whatever is down below. It spots him. It barks, pounds its knuckles on the ground, bares its teeth, and runs toward him. In a flash, the boy seizes the key to the big cage, opens it, and drags Scuttle out.

Holmes wonders if the baboon is just threatening him. But instantly, the big creature is after them. Sherlock snaps his whip in its face and it jumps back, but then immediately advances again. Holmes is desperate to get to the pit and see what is harbored down there, but his first thoughts are for Scuttle. The little boy is barely conscious and seems frighteningly weak. *I must get him out of here!* Holmes keeps his face to his tormentor, his right arm under Scuttle's arms and across his scrawny chest, dragging him, backing away in the direction of the passage, cracking his whip while he goes. As Sherlock reaches the tunnel, the giant ape stops: *it must never go down the passage.* Before long, they are far apart – the boy hears the big baboon barking in the distance, its outline evident in the light.

Holmes has to move in the dark the rest of the way, pulling his load. He had feared he couldn't even do this on his own. But anxious to save the little one he has put into danger, he finds the strength and courage he needs, and soon, is at the iron door. He left it slightly ajar. He pulls it open and slams it behind him, locking it. Then he drags Scuttle out onto the beach and puts him down on the mud. He turns toward the water. Breathing heavily, his heart still racing, he puts his hands on his knees, and vomits.

Sherlock Holmes sits on the mud for a long time after that, Scuttle beside him, still moaning. Finally, he gets to his feet and cups some water from the Thames in his hands and gently splashes it in his friend's face. The small boy's eyes focus a little, and he appears, for the first time, to actually look at Sherlock. But he doesn't speak. It seems as though he can't.

"Scuttle, can you hear me?"

The other boy nods.

"I am going to take you to see an apothecary."

The boy grips him by the hand, so hard that he almost cracks his finger bones.

"I will stay with you."

His grip lessens.

All the way into central London, Scuttle says nothing. It is strange to be with this talkative boy and not hear him utter a word. There is a haunted look in his eyes, as if he has seen something terrible, and it is still with him. He walks but does so like a ghost, floating at Sherlock's side, his feather-weight propped up as they move. They stick to the smaller avenues, and when they reach the bottom of Denmark Street, the bigger boy stops and gets back into his disguise – boots inside his reversed frock coat, bare feet, a stoop to decrease his height, all to go with his still muddied face and hair. He takes Scuttle's arm again, and together they approach the apothecary shop.

As expected, a Bobbie stands nearby, resplendent in his long, buttoned-down blue coat and helmet. He is slapping a truncheon against his hand. The two boys stumble directly past him. Neither of them matches the description of young Master Holmes.

Sherlock has the presence of mind to knock.

Irene answers the door, holding it open a crack. "Yes?" she asks. Beatrice is right behind her. "It's you!" she cries out. The door opens, and they are brought inside.

As Holmes gets out of his disguise, Scuttle is laid on the laboratory table, and Sigerson Bell begins to perform his own sort of magic. He starts by giving the little lad a good snort from a bottle of gin.

"These two young ladies appeared here this afternoon and proclaimed that they hadn't seen you, my boy, for some time, one, since this morning – *imagine that* – and were concerned. They have ensconced themselves here ever since, anxiously awaiting your arrival."

"Not *that* anxiously, sir," insists Miss Doyle, "I simply have something to tell him." Miss Leckie remains quiet, glowing at Sherlock.

The boy looks enquiringly at Irene.

"What I have to say . . . can wait," she says, looking at Scuttle.

"As for me," says the apothecary, "I shall bring this child back to life – a good hot flask of my special tea and a serving of cold mutton should do most of the trick, though we will resort to toad bile if we must. And you, my young knight, shall tell us who this lad is, why he is the way he is, and what you have been up to. I see your whip has been in use." Bell's keen eye has spotted it hanging partially out of Holmes's sleeve, its butt covered with mud.

The old man raises Scuttle to a sitting position and twists him in all sorts of ways, asking him to breathe deeply while he does. As Sherlock begins to talk, Scuttle is fed some of the tea that the three have been drinking (though the apothecary adds another splash of gin to the little boy's) and great slabs of mutton and several scones. Both Irene and Beatrice tend to him with gentle care, a fact that seems to contribute substantially to his rapid improvement. He looks more like himself within minutes. Still, he doesn't speak.

Sherlock explains about his adventures, which have stretched now into the late afternoon. All his listeners are riveted. Beatrice looks upset, Irene shocked, and Sigerson Bell absolutely fascinated. His eyes sparkle, and his body contorts as the action is described, as if he were fighting off the baboon himself.

"Excellent! Excellent, my young knight! Had I been there I would have administered a little Bellitsu to that simian monster, boxed its ears and dropped kicked him whilst you were diverting him with your whip-snapping prowess!" The image of this ancient, bent-over man in mortal combat with a baboon is almost enough to make Sherlock smile, even as he tells his desperate tale. So intense is his audience that they have all begun to ignore poor Scuttle, who sits on the lab table behind them munching on his third scone. As Sherlock comes to the part that describes the breathtaking escape onto the beach, they hear a little voice behind them.

"In the servicement of clarification, might I give some relations as to what occurred to Scuttle in the extremely small hours of this morning?"

They all turn to him. Sherlock, especially, is relieved to hear him speak.

"When this agent of Scottish Yard, 'ere –" continues the little boy, pointing at Holmes, "and I am making assumptions that you ladies and this nubile old wizard are also under the covers with the London Metropollution Police Force – encountered yours truly on guard outside The World's End 'otel, where he is known to speak with many famous celebritants, an ass-signment was given, without the 'elp of a badge, to go down into the secret chambers and solve a mystery."

"Scuttle," says Sherlock, "I have related all of that. Please tell us what happened once you were inside."

"Well, sir, I opened the wall, as your secret instructioning instructed me to do. My 'eart was sweating and my 'ands pounding. I could 'ear with my ears noises in another chamber, as you sir, agent of Scottish Yard, had imitated there might be. There was awful screeching and screaming and sounds that might make a man throw up his victuals from his bowels out onto the ground. I moved toward it . . . though not at lightning speed, I'd say, due to a knocking about of my knees. It was dark and I could not see with my eyes what was transporting in that chamber. And then, a bad thing 'appened."

"A bad thing?" asks Irene.

"Scuttle fell."

"You fell?"

"Just at the opening to the lower chamber, and rolled like a rolling pin down the stairs. Scuttle is not always a ballet man on his feet."

"I can imagine," says Bell sympathetically.

"And there they were . . . and Scuttle directly amidst them."

"They?" asks Sherlock.

"Two men."

"Who?"

"I think, sir, that one was 'emsworth."

Irene gasps.

"You think?" asks Sherlock.

"Well, one thing Scuttle 'as never really said . . . is that I at no times actually viewed Mr. 'emsworth's face with my own eyeballs, though I felt I 'ad seen 'im in the dark many times at the Cremorne. I 'ad related that I gabbed with 'im . . . but that was not strictly the truthful truth. And underground, 'e pulled 'is 'at down low too, when 'is eyeballs fiercely saw me, as if to say to me that 'e was under the covers as well."

"Who was the other man?"

"A man I 'ad viewed, once or twice, in the Gardens."

"Wearing a black greatcoat?" asks Irene.

"The wery one! You are an agent of some greatness."

"What happened next?" asks Beatrice.

"Scuttle was full of nervousment, seeing all the creatures in there, many seeming to be sweating their 'earts out, and they was screaming and the like . . . rats and monkeys and pigs, all in cages. There was a big cage too, with stains of blood in it. The two men 'ad just come up a ramp that went down into a pit, which I couldn't see into. They 'ad an entire coach, a black one that looked like it was built by many midgets it was so low, but still long, and they 'ad four big 'orses pulling it too, right there in the cave. Scuttle felt like he was in a story by that Edgar Ellen Pow, who writes of terrible things containing ghosts and dead people and the like. Well, the two men didn't seem too pleasured to meet me, at least not at first, but then their smiles came up on their visagings, and one said to the other that I would be perfect."

"For what?" asks Bell, looking like he knows the answer.

"Well, old nubile wizard, I figured it soon enough. They decided . . . they wanted . . ." The boy's voice falters and his eyes redden.

"They were considering feeding you to whatever they were keeping in the pit," says Sherlock.

Scuttle nods and breaks down, sobbing.

"You have said enough," says Beatrice and pats him on the shoulder. Irene, whose face has turned very white, takes his hand.

"Scuttle can go on," says the little boy, gathering himself. "They put me in the big cage, where I stayed without water or sustenancing until this agent of Scottish Yard saved me with much valor. I was not able to give myself private relief, no urine nation or things of a larger nature, as I am sorry to relate in this mixed-up company. The two men took the 'orses and all and left out the passage this agent arrived from in the morning. Then, a few hours after they excavated the premises, the baboon . . . 'e started feeding the beast . . . other poor animals . . . from the other cages."

Sherlock gets to his feet, his eyes on fire, holding his hands to his temples as he talks and walks. He doesn't look bored, not at all. "The Hemsworth show takes place every other day. That is unusual, and by design. I've wondered about it for a while, but now I understand. It is so he and Riyah can do the following: feed this beast, which they own together, move it only at night, and have it hungry at just the right times."

"I doesn't follow you, my agent," says Scuttle.

"You will recall, Irene, that backstage and in the hallways of the theater while Hemsworth is in residence, there are very few people about. In fact, other than Venus, who leaves the moment she is done, and the ten musicians who appear to gather up their instruments and depart out the front doors, there is no one."

"Why is that significant? Aren't magicians secretive?" asks Beatrice. "Doesn't it make sense that they don't want others around their carefully guarded tricks and equipment?"

"But not *that* secretive!" exclaims Bell, "It is a front, for something they are hiding."

"They are keeping the beast," Sherlock continues, "somewhere in the bowels of The Egyptian Hall and forbidding anyone to come near it. But it isn't left alone in its cage down there for long after each show, just until about three o'clock in the morning."

"When Riyah and Hemsworth pick it up at the back door," says Bell.

"Yes. They take it, chained and restricted, as hungry as a lion since it hasn't been fed all day – which means it is nasty and aggressive during its time onstage – and take it through the London night in nearly deserted streets and along back alleys . . . until they get to that singular little road that leads down to the beach at the Battersea Bridge."

"Something Hemsworth must have discovered about the time he learned of the triple-chambered basement under The World's End Hotel nearby!" cries Bell.

"Or perhaps the owner, the shadowy Riyah, knew about it and about the passage that leads from the quiet beach there into the third chamber with the pit."

"Excellent!" shouts the old man, almost in admiration of the two cruel men.

"They then take the beast into the secret chamber, closing and camouflaging the opening behind, and put it carefully into the pit, in a strong cage."

"Then they feeds it, my agent."

"Yes. And whatever it is, it has a ferocious appetite. It likes to eat living things, of any size. Those pigs and monkeys don't seem to be the largest of its meals. It will eat prey that can fight back, and yet easily kills and devours them. I saw no bones, not even large quantities of blood in that chamber. I think it eats everything, skull and all."

"Like it did with Nottingham!" declares Bell.

His comment silences everyone for a moment.

"I'm sorry," whispers Irene.

"It isn't reasonable," continues Sherlock, "for Hemsworth and Riyah to be in the secret chambers day after day, tending to the beast, and they don't want to be seen there in broad daylight, anyway. So, they leave after they deposit it and feed it. But it wants its flesh and blood regularly."

"So . . . the baboon feeds it," says Scuttle.

"Yes . . . they have taught him how, likely in exchange for tasty meals of his own. They come back and get the beast on the second day, in the middle of the night, before the following day's performance. They hide it at The Egyptian Hall again and don't feed it until show time, as I said, so it is ferocious when it needs to be. Then, the whole cycle begins again."

"I . . . I am sorry about defending Hemsworth," says Irene clearly.

"So did I, Miss Doyle," responds Sherlock, "right to Lestrade's face."

"I . . . I am singing tomorrow night . . . for him."

"Perfect," says Sherlock.

"What do you mean?"

"You can get me backstage, where I can look around, where I can confront them."

"I'll do whatever has to be done. But are you going in there alone?"

"I will bring Mr. Bell with me." The apothecary beams. "And the police will be there, too."

"The police? But they won't come, Sherlock, not for you, and not after what happened the last time they attended."

"It won't be like that tomorrow night. The last time, Riyah knew I had spoken to the Lestrades. I am sure that I saw him near Scotland Yard. Hemsworth mentioned several times to me that day that he knew I was coming, even that I had 'friends' coming – he meant the police. Riyah warned His Highness, and they faked the dragon that night – they must have the means to do that, in case they are inspected. But Irene, you can use your charms again, to get Lestrade's son to come to the theater."

"He won't fall for that twice."

"Yes, he will. Tomorrow is different: you have a legitimate reason to ask him. Just send your card round to the police headquarters today, tell him that you are making your great debut and you would like him there. He won't be able to resist that. Ask him to bring a friend. It will almost certainly be another policeman."

"But, my agent, won't Mr. 'emsworth notice when 'e and Mr. Riyah come to the pit of evil tonight, that I is . . . escaped?"

"No, Scuttle, they would not expect you to be there."

"They wouldn't?"

"You must understand their schedule. Yes, they will return to the chamber in the black hours tonight to get their creature. But before that, the big baboon intended to drag you to the pit . . . it would be about now, in fact . . . after you had weakened more. You would have been fed, while you were still alive . . . to the dragon."

Irene forgets all about what she came to tell Sherlock.

HEMSWORTH'S CONFESSION

Morning comes, and thankfully the shop isn't searched.

They all attend the Hemsworth spectacle that evening. Irene gets them tickets: Sherlock, Bell, Beatrice, Scuttle (eyes as wide as saucers and dressed in a new shirt and trousers that Irene provides for him), Andrew C. Doyle (looking slightly embarrassed that his daughter is singing, but trying to take a modern view), and his adopted son, little Paul, dressed in imitation of his father.

The apothecary has armed both himself and his apprentice with horsewhips. The old man will keep his secreted up his underclothing inside that pink outfit, ready for action in his seat ten rows from the stage and close to an aisle.

But Holmes doesn't sit in the audience. Dressed in disguise on the way, and presented to the theater attendants as an escort for Miss Doyle, he arrives early with her and slips down the hallway past Hemsworth's dressing room, reluctantly leaving her with him. She had insisted that she was not frightened.

I hope I won't regret this.

He had noticed during his first visit backstage that there was a door at the end of the hallway, past the dressing rooms. He makes for it. As he suspects, it leads downstairs into the basement, the perfect place to keep the dragon. The staircase is narrow and creaky, hardly steps one could negotiate with a huge beast in tow. But that isn't how it is moved. *If the creature is down here, then it is taken directly to and from this basement by way of that big stable door behind the theater.* The only thing that doesn't make sense is the fact that the back door is at street level, and he is presently descending below it.

When he gets to the bottom of the stairs, he under-stands. It is dark in here, but not totally black. He looks straight up to the ceiling and sees many little lines of bright light above. *The stage!* He is directly below it. To his left, a hallway leads from this room up to another few lines of light, four of them, two vertical and two horizontal . . . *the stable door at the back of the theater!* There must be a ramp there. To his right, the room slants up in darkness . . . *where the orchestra pit and the audience must be.* He hears some-thing moving in the cavernous room. There is a hiss, like the sound a huge snake might make. He freezes. Something large is moving, thrashing about, no more than fifty feet away, directly under the stage. Sherlock feels for his horse-whip in his sleeve.

At that instant someone seizes him, someone big and powerful, and instantly he is dragged back up the stairs. In the commotion, he thinks he hears a cry in the room below. It sounds like a child or a woman. But in seconds, he is back up to the top of the stairs, the door is slammed behind him, and he is pitched down the hallway toward Hemsworth's dressing room.

Before him stands Oscar Riyah.

His first instinct is to run. His second is to apply a little Bellitsu. But he doesn't. *I have to see this out . . . now. I can't go, anyway. Irene is in the dressing room. I can't leave her there.*

"Mr. Sherlock Holmes."

The boy tries to remember if he ever told Riyah his full name.

"What a pleasure to see you," adds the old Jew. His accent seems to be faltering.

"The pleasure is all mine, sir. You have been avoiding me, and the police."

"Not at all, we are just waiting for ze opportune moment. Might you step into my colleague's dressing room for a chat?" He shoves Sherlock toward the door, opens it, pushes him inside, and enters too. Irene sits at a dressing table with a mirror, fixing her face, Hemsworth beside her, doing the same. She is trying not to look nervous, but when Sherlock enters, she jumps to her feet.

"Miss Doyle," says Sherlock calmly. "I hear you are singing this evening."

"Dispense with the charade, Holmes. You suspect me, don't you?"

"No."

"No?" Hemsworth almost looks concerned.

"It is far beyond suspicion, sir. I know you murdered the Wizard of Nottingham and I know how you did it."

Riyah snickers.

"And you, sir," exclaims the boy, turning on the man in the greatcoat, "you are part of this, for whatever evil reason, and shall be hanged with him."

"Well," sighs Hemsworth, getting to his feet. "We have you in an enclosed space. As far as you know, we are armed, perhaps with better weapons than horsewhips."

Holmes swallows.

"And we have the young lady, too. What might we do to her, right now . . . in your presence?"

Sherlock thinks of the stories of Hemsworth's cruelty. There is a glint in his eye. He is growing excited. He is, indeed, mad. He has fed living animals to his creature, and was about to do the same with poor Scuttle.

"I have been to your studio – all the way in. I can direct the police there."

"Well done!" exclaims Riyah, without a trace of the German accent.

"Yes, indeed, impressive," adds Hemsworth. "But, you see, in order to accomplish such heroics, you would have to get out of here alive. We may not simply want to escape. We might not only be planning to do something deliciously horrible to Miss Doyle, but we may also have plans for you. So, you will not be able to direct the police anywhere, young sleuth. Now, what could we do to you? Ah, yes: we could feed you, alive, to . . ." He pauses.

Irene steps toward Sherlock, her face pale, and takes him by the arm. She glares at the men. *She is brave indeed.*

"But no, we are honorable men, are we not . . . Riyah?"

"Most certainly, your Highness. We believe in justice. Justice shall be served here . . . as surely as it is in a Dickens novel."

The two men laugh.

A light comes on in Sherlock's brain. *This Mr. Riyah DOES have a false name. Maybe two.* Bell's favorite Dickens novel is *Our Mutual Friend*, the great author's latest. He reads it constantly, often out loud and with, regrettably, great feeling, shouting and acting out the characters. *Of course! The name of the Jew in* Our Mutual Friend, . . . *is Riah.* Sherlock recalls that his father had said something about this man's other name – Abraham Hebrewitz – sounding like it came from a book. *I should have made the connection then! If Lestrade, that fool, read more than* The Illustrated Police News, *he would have known too! This man in the greatcoat, whoever he really is, plucked at least one of his identities from the pages of Dickens' latest novel . . . and then hinted at it right in front of me! They are toying with us. They think this is a game, a piece of theater. Murder and cruelty is a game to them!*

"So, being two fair and just gentlemen . . ." continues Hemsworth, "we shall turn ourselves in to you and the Metropolitan London Police!"

Sherlock's mouth drops open. "You what?"

"Of course, my boy. Yes, I did the murderous deed, though I shall not tell you or anyone else exactly how."

"I know how."

"Oh, you do, do you? Be that as it may, let me say that I eliminated him in the cause of justice. I was wronged! And I received my justice! My vengeance!" His face turns red. "But I have been fairly caught, and that is to be respected. I promised myself I would accept my punishment should I be truly found out."

"Come with me, sir," says Sherlock, "we shall cancel the show."

"No."

"No?"

"The show must go on. The show must always go on." He holds an arm in the air and shouts. "The public must have it!"

"I don't think that it –"

"It is my last request. I insist! In fact, if you do not allow this . . . I shall dispense with both you and Miss Doyle ahead of time."

Sherlock and Irene look at each other. She squeezes his hand.

"But that shouldn't be necessary. Miss Doyle shall sing! She must have her great moment! You will stay locked in here, Holmes, simply to ensure that you will not interfere. But I promise you, on my word and the word of Mr. Riyah . . ."

"Absolutely," says the other man earnestly.

"That we will turn ourselves in to the police when the curtain falls."

"And your creature?"

"What creature? Master Holmes, you are a fantasist, which is surprising, since I had heard you were so rational, so practical, and so scientific about everything."

How does he know anything about me?

"There is no creature. Surely, the police saw that last time?"

"I know you are harboring something."

"Of what sort? A dragon?" He and Riyah laugh out loud. Hemsworth stops suddenly and looks at Sherlock with a grin. "You are falling for my tricks!"

"I don't know exactly what it is that you —"

"Well, if you don't know, then you should not open your mouth! And besides, even if you were correct, is it a crime to keep a pet, however large or aggressive? I have transported many beasts from Africa, the Holy Land, and the Orient. I have sold them to respectable people here at home. That is not criminal activity. And it is not a crime to feed them, either. . . . . There is no creature, anyway." He gets to his feet. "Master Holmes, you may not find my word credible, considering what I did, but I say again: I promise you I will be available to the police when the show ends. I promise you! I did what I did for the right reasons, and I am willing to pay the price. I got everything I wanted." The look on his face is earnest, and Sherlock, despite reservations, believes him.

But that doesn't stop Holmes from wanting to be sure, from seeking a way out of his tiny prison. The second that Hemsworth, Irene, and Riyah leave the room, locking it behind them, the boy is up and examining the door and its latch. But try as he might, he can't open it from the inside. He employs his little wire and works on it for some time, but it seems to be constructed differently from a regular lock.

He sits down at the chair Irene had been using and looks into the mirror. He fixes his hair, straightens his collar, knocks the lint from his shoulders, then looks at himself in both profiles and tries to figure out which makes him most handsome, most manly. "My nose is too big," he says, fascinated as he watches himself speak. He turns his head a little bit farther in profile, so the nose looks smaller. "That's better."

He sighs. *So, Hemsworth admits it.*

Sherlock has come to the end of another case, not one he wanted to be part of in the first place. Despite his high opinion of his own intelligence, what he has accomplished while just a lad still amazes him. He must truly have a talent for this. And perhaps he has been fortunate. But he may not be if he tries anything like this again, before he is better prepared.

He hears Irene's voice. It begins to soar in the theater, the new opening for Hemsworth's great show. He is taken aback by how beautifully she sings. *Yes, that is the career for her.* It is a song about magic, about dragons, and jealousy, and fame. He wants to see her sing it. It is ridiculous that he is cooped up in here. He goes back to the lock and tries it again but cannot spring it.

Sherlock sits down with a thud. Time passes and he hears the music end for the first act. He paces during the intermission and then sits at the dressing table once more as the second act begins. He recalls that it is much shorter than the first.

Looking at the boy in the mirror, he can see his mother's eyes. "I keep putting people, people I care about, into peril." He thinks of Irene, who cannot be for him, of Beatrice who perhaps should be, of Scuttle, who was almost fed, alive, to a vicious animal. "This life I am choosing can't have many friendships, any love." But even now, Sherlock Holmes feels a deep-seated fascination for the very danger he is worrying about. He can't hold it back. He thinks of the beast in the basement. "I believe everything Hemsworth told me," he tells his image, "because it makes sense. But why is he lying about the creature? Or is he? How else could His Highness have killed the Wizard?"

He gets to his feet. The show will be done soon. *What if Hemsworth is lying about tonight too? What if he is planning to slip away? I must get out of here.*

He reminds himself that there are still many other things unsolved about this case – who is Mr. Riyah, for example, and where, *exactly*, is Mrs. Nottingham? Even if Hemsworth does turn himself in, will he reveal everything, or does he even know where his former wife is? Will Riyah vanish again, and will the "dragon" magically disappear too?

There is even something unsolved about this very room. He looks around. Riyah was in here, he is sure, both the first time he and Irene visited, and the time they came back. *Why was he hiding? What is his role in all of this? Did he have a reason to hate Nottingham too? Significant enough to help murder him?* Sherlock doesn't care what Lestrade says, the "old Jew" was in here. The police must have missed something when they searched the room. A Hemsworth trick was at work.

He surveys his surroundings. The curtain, behind which Sherlock thought Riyah hid, is gone, and a blank wall remains. He thinks of Bell saying that magicians don't perform real magic. There is always a rational solution to their mysteries. The room is small, containing just the two dressing tables with mirrors, a settee for guests, and a clothing rack where various costumes are hung. Riyah could not have hidden behind the rack: none of the costumes touch the floor, so his feet would have shown beneath them. The boy examines the walls. He runs his hands along them from top to bottom and side to side, covering every inch. All four are solid.

Be rational, be practical. If Hemsworth and Riyah could find a way through any of the surfaces in this room, which one would they choose? The walls? *Why? They simply lead to other rooms.* The ceiling? *Maybe, but it would just take you to the roof.* The floor? *Of course . . . the floor!* There is a rug on it, covering almost the entire surface, hiding any exit. *And what is beneath it? The basement . . . where the beast is held!* It's perfect. Sherlock gets onto his knees and rolls the rug back, then examines the floor as carefully as he can, nose close to it, eyeing the edges of every board, wishing he had Bell's spyglass. He is almost done when he finds two boards cut slightly shorter than all the others, near the wall, to the right as someone enters the room . . . *to the right . . . that's the same direction one must go to pass along the hallway to the staircase that leads down to the part of the basement that is under the stage.*

But it's no use. The boards aren't loose. The gap between them and the others is infinitesimal – he can barely get his fingernails between them. They won't budge.

Sherlock stands up. He isn't sure what to do now. *Will I have to wait here until the show is over? What if I am being played for a fool and all is lost?* He thinks of what His Highness said to him . . . "*You are falling for my tricks.*"

He sits at Hemsworth's dressing table this time. *Never give up.* He looks down at the table top. *What did Irene and I used to say?* "We need to eliminate the things that couldn't possibly have happened, and work on the things that are most likely." *So, the answer isn't in the room's surfaces. Where else could it be?* He examines the dressing table and realizes that the top opens. Inside, he sees tubes of stage makeup in piles. He shoves them back, seeking the bottom of the drawer. There is a book down there. He looks at the title . . . *The Existence of Dragons!* He opens it. *Blank pages.* He flips through them, all the way to the end. The book is nailed down and after the last page, it is just a frame. Right there, in that frame, a small lever sticks up. *His Highness has such flair!* Sherlock glances under the desk and sees a column attached to it, connecting it to the floor. He looks at the lever again, and pulls on it. It won't move. He pulls it harder. It snaps down and he hears a whirring sound behind him. He turns around.

The two short floorboards near the right wall are sliding back!

In a flash, he is stepping beneath them. His feet come to rest on a false floor in a narrow tunnel, about a yard high and wide. He has to go down on his hands and knees to get his head beneath the floor but when he does, he sees that the passage leads to the right, at a slight angle . . . in the direction of the basement room.

He crawls forward and soon wonders exactly where he is: perhaps moving below the other dressing rooms now. It isn't far from Hemsworth's location to the basement door at the end of the hallway, maybe forty or fifty feet. After he has crawled about half that distance, he hears something. It is coming from above. He rolls onto his back and looks up. He can see through a half-inch crack in the floorboards, directly into another room. He squints. Someone is in there, getting dressed. When he focuses, he can tell it is Venus . . . her entire body from the waist up is clearly visible in the crack . . . and she isn't getting dressed . . . *she's undressing*. He gawks at her. She is wearing her skimpy, nearly see-through muslin costume, much of her body exposed. He notices her out-of-doors evening clothes lying on a table next to her. She is indeed a magnetic woman, even more so than usual at this moment, while slipping off her clothes. Sherlock can't take his eyes from her. He knows he shouldn't be looking. But he is fighting his fifteen . . . nearly sixteen-year-old chemistry. She has no way of knowing he is here. *I can watch. No one would know. She won't know.* She is peeling off the muslin, her beautiful dark skin showing on her lithe arms and slim neck . . . a vision. Sherlock sees the top of the white underclothing that covers her chest. She is about to take that off too. . . . He clenches his teeth, summons his strength, and finds his sense of right and wrong. *No one would know . . . except me.* He turns his eyes away, rolls over, and moves on.

In another twenty feet, the passage comes to a dead end. But when he presses on the little, cut out section of wall in front of him, it pushes open. He is at the landing on the staircase, above the basement at the end of the hallway.

Once again, he hears something hissing and thrashing below . . . something large.

SHOWSTOPPER

Holmes descends the stairs in the direction of the sounds. He can hear the band in the orchestra pit to his right, the audience reacting out in front of it, and Hemsworth's voice, as clear as a bell.

"This is the night of nights for our show."

Our show? Has he ever called it that before?

"This is the greatest night of magic in the history of the London stage, in the history of magic anywhere! On this first day of September 1869, we will shock the world!"

He was always a humble man. He won't be so proud when he is sitting in jail awaiting his justice!

Sherlock has reached the bottom of the stairs. He takes a few careful steps and sees a cage, about twenty feet away, barely discernable in the darkness, about the size of the one used for the dragon on show nights. Something is inside, making that hissing sound, and thrashing about. But he can't figure out what it is, yet. He edges closer. It lunges at him . . . and he sees it!

A gigantic lizard! A monstrous reptile!

It snaps at the bars of the cage, just inches from the boy. Its big face is confronting him, eyes as black as a crow, huge, razor-sharp teeth bared. Sherlock jerks back and its forked tongue snakes out almost a foot, nearly touching his cheek. Several feet away, in an instant cold sweat, he stares at it in disbelief. It had reared up, but now it drops down again, coiling itself as if to make another lunge. Green-gray, with a six-foot-long body and a four-foot tale, it looks heavier than a fully grown man. There are fake wings attached to its back, where it can't reach behind and rip them off. *It wants to kill me.* But Sherlock can see, up this close, that its legs are shackled. Thick ropes, like those used to moor an enormous ship, hold the lizard to the back of the cage. *That's why it can't get at Venus.*

Where, in God's name, did Hemsworth find this creature? Deep in the jungles of Africa? In the deserts of the Holy Land? On a distant island in the Indian Ocean? Sherlock remembers Bell telling him that there may be dinosaur-like beings somewhere on earth, and that there is more in this world than is dreamt of in his imagination. *There certainly is.*

"Dragon, are you ready?" says a voice in a whisper.

Sherlock starts and freezes, then silently slips away in the darkness and plasters himself against a wall a few carriage lengths away.

It is Riyah. He is holding a small lantern, directed at the ground, so he can find his way. He carries an axe in his hand. He drops it near the big ship ropes. His voice sounds different. It is rich and mellifluous, almost theatrical, even as he whispers. There is absolutely no hint of a German accent.

"This is our big night, our special night," he says to the beast, keeping his voice low. "You will have to wait a little longer this evening, dragon. But it will be worth it. You will get your prize onstage this time. Yes, you can have it tonight!"

The voice sounds vaguely familiar. He imagines it at full volume. It is beginning to dawn on Sherlock whom Oscar Riyah may be, and the possibility is startling him right out of his trousers. *It can't be!*

"Come here!" he hears Riyah hiss. Sherlock looks toward the little spotlight the lantern is casting in the darkness. Riyah has Venus in his filthy hands. *She has gotten here so quickly!* It is difficult to see her face, but it is obvious, even from where he is, that white makeup has been applied to every inch of her skin that is visible, and there is a good deal of that. She has a crown on her head, the purple Egyptian robe too, though it is wide open, displaying that skimpy muslin outfit underneath, nearly see-through, showing much of her body, and fitting tightly to her shape. Her hands are tied behind her back now, her eyes blindfolded, her mouth gagged. She struggles against him. *Why is he doing this? They are backstage and the audience can't see her! She knows what she has to do. Why does he have to force her? Does it really scare her that much? But she told me that she didn't even see the dragon, and didn't seem to care about it.*

Riyah takes her around to the front of the cage, opens a door there and shoves her in, securing the door behind her with a small lock. It will hold *her* in, but not the dragon: another reason it is shackled. She clings to the bars at the front of the cage, as far away from the beast as possible. It comes forward a foot or so, its big front claws moving up onto a short ramp between them, elevating the front of its body, making it look more like a slightly upright dragon, than a huge, low-to-the-ground monitor lizard. *Very clever.* But it can't get any closer to her. It darts its forked tongue in her direction.

Sherlock thinks again of how quickly Venus must change from one outfit to the next. She is an efficient, seasoned professional. But then something else occurs to him. He remembers the riveting sight of the beautiful "African princess" undressing in her room. Beside her, on a table, he had glimpsed her outdoor clothing. That, obviously, was what she was about to put on . . . not what she is wearing now in the cage. He realizes, too, that because he had been so enthralled by her beauty and the excitement of the moment, it hadn't even dawned on him that it made no sense for her to be taking *off* that nearly see-through outfit. *Taking it off! How could she have been taking it off . . . if she was about to wear it under the robe inside the cage?*

Sherlock moves as fast and as silently as he can back to the staircase and up it. He opens the little door at the landing and gets down into the passageway, scurrying back along it on his hands and feet until he comes to Venus's room. He turns over and looks up. She is still there! And fully dressed in her outdoor clothing, Juliet again, sticking the last pin in her hat! She vanishes from his sightline toward the hallway.

She isn't the princess in peril! It isn't her in the cage! But then . . . who is it?

Sherlock rushes frantically back down the passageway toward the landing. When he opens the little door and stands up, he can't see the spotlight near the cage. Riyah has disappeared. Then he hears Hemsworth's baritone booming in the theater, sounding excited.

"I told you this was the night of nights for magic!"

Sherlock spots Riyah, racing up a series of winding stairs against the wall on the other side of the room, spotlight bouncing in front of him. Those stairs go up to the stage. Riyah is throwing off his greatcoat, revealing a glittering costume, pulling off a long-haired wig, ripping away his beard, putting on his spectacles.

"I am going to bring to conclusion, right here on our stage tonight," exclaims His Highness, "the greatest illusion in the history of the world. They said I murdered the Wizard of Nottingham. I did not. Tonight . . . I shall . . . BRING HIM BACK TO LIFE!"

Riyah is Nottingham!

Sherlock hears the audience gasp. The Wizard is standing before them, returned from the dead, emerging out of darkness at the wave of His Highness's hand. *Hemsworth, indeed, did not murder his rival. He has been working with him. Those bits of flesh came from an animal.* "You are falling for my tricks," that was what His Highness told him. Now Sherlock knows what it really meant. *But it wasn't just a trick, it was an elaborate web of tricks, focused on manipulating public opinion, on employing Sherlock Holmes and Irene Doyle and Inspector Lestrade and the Metropolitan London Police Force and every newspaper in the city . . . as actors in the illusion. It was coughs and fluttering curtains and secret chambers; it was adjustable hats marked with initials.* The audience is thundering its applause, stamping its feet. Nottingham has been using Hemsworth and his creature to perform his greatest trick. They both have their *revenge*.

But when Sherlock thinks of that word he thinks of Venus's verbal portrait of her boss, the one she painted on the streets that night not long ago. She said he was a beast, cruel and vicious, intent on fame, and that Nottingham was just as bad. He thinks of what she said about the woman who left both of them: that she was a free spirit, that she seduced Nottingham, and then found others more desirable than the Wizard. She has a weakness for men. She crossed these two proud men *publicly* . . . they, whom no one should cross. Holmes thinks of Juliet saying that Hemsworth often spoke of the gruesome ways he would like to murder his philandering former wife.

So . . . Mrs. Nottingham has vanished, has she?

Sherlock looks across the dark room to the white woman in the cage with the giant lizard. He sees her holding on to the bars at the far end of her prison, her mouth gagged, eyes blindfolded . . . terrified. *Mrs. Nottingham!* Then Sherlock remembers the axe that the Wizard had in his hands just a few minutes ago. He dropped it near the big ship ropes that hold the dragon back, keep it from attacking anything that might be in its cage.

"And now, for the great moment!" Shouts the Wizard up on the stage. "But tonight it will be more real than ever before! Tonight, look, if you dare, at the greatest, most violent, most gruesome illusion the world has ever seen! You shall see its CONCLUSION!"

The audience is alive with excitement, getting to their feet, aware that they are about to see something extraordinary, even greater than the dragon trick itself, created in tandem by a Far East adventurer and the greatest magician in the world.

"Appear dragon!" cries His Highness.

The band strikes up and suddenly a section of the floor of the basement begins to lift toward the stage, raising the famished dragon and Mrs. Nottingham with it. Part of the stage shifts back to allow the cage to rise. Sherlock, glued to a wall, stares up.

"You will get your prize onstage this time." That's what Nottingham had whispered to the dragon. "Yes, you can have it tonight!"

They are going to feed their philandering wife to the giant lizard on the stage of The Egyptian Hall! There will be blood, crunching of bones, screams, and an unparalleled sensation . . . gruesome reality at its finest, an illusion for the ages . . . but not really an illusion. There will be nothing left of her! And no evidence!

Sherlock has no weapon but his horsewhip. He races across the basement, falling into wooden boxes and picking himself up. He leaps onto the winding staircase at the other side of the room and flies upward toward the stage. When he arrives, he sees Hemsworth standing at stage left, Nottingham by the ropes with his axe in hand. The dragon is hissing, striving with all its might to get at its living meal. She is screaming underneath her gag. She knows what is about to happen.

"Your Highness?" shouts Nottingham and turns to his partner.

"Tonight," intones Hemsworth on cue, "it shall not be as in days of old. No saint will save the lady. She shall be *devoured*!!!" His voice has grown evil.

An old man in a bizarre pink outfit, bent in the shape of a question mark, is rising to his feet in the tenth row to get to the stage.

There are two ship ropes. Nottingham rears back and slashes at the first. It doesn't slice through.

Sherlock makes for him, but the Wizard's second swing severs the rope and the dragon lunges forward. His human prey clings to the bars, just inches from the end of the flicking tongue. Nottingham's back is to Holmes; he doesn't see him. The magician moves away from the boy toward the other rope and gets a swing at it before Sherlock nears. Holmes won't reach him before he makes his second swing! The beast will be loosed! It will kill and consume Mrs. Nottingham in front of The Egyptian Hall crowd! They are all now on their feet and most are applauding wildly, cheering on Nottingham and the dragon.

Holmes snaps his horsewhip from his sleeve and cracks it at the Wizard. His aim is off and the cord misses the axe . . . but wraps around Nottingham's arm . . . *the wrong arm*. Looking at the boy in surprise, the magician still has the presence of mind to bring the axe down on the rope with his free arm. *It severs.*

Sigerson Trismegistus Bell is well aware of what is reality and what is illusion at this moment. Over the last few minutes, his big brain has been processing many of the same things his assistant has been considering below the stage.

He, too, has calculated all that is planned to transpire in front of the audience as he races down the aisle and leaps onto the stage. Irene and Beatrice are behind him. Both young ladies, dresses and all, make the leap too.

The band stops playing, its members stare up at the scene in front of them.

Bell eyes both the big scimitar blade (hanging in midair – actually from a black cord – where it was left after the decapitation scene) and the little lock on the cage door in front of the terrified woman. He rips the sword from its cord and darts to the cage. Just as Nottingham severs the last rope, just as the huge lizard rushes for the woman, Bell brings the weapon down on the lock with tremendous force and smashes it apart. He opens the door in a flash, and pulls the woman out, saving her from the lunging lizard by inches.

The crowd erupts in thunderous cheers, rocking the theater.

But the famished reptile is still making for her. It has slithered over its ramp and gotten to the door with alarming speed. Now, it tries to burst through the tight space and out onto the stage. Its tongue goes through, then its head . . . but nothing else. It writhes in the doorway and hisses, potential human meals reflected in its shiny black eyes.

As Hemsworth and Nottingham look on in disbelief, the audience roars again with delight.

If it gets through, it will kill whomever it encounters!

But Sigerson Bell has had enough. He turns to the crowd, wielding his big gleaming blade over his head like a crazed warrior. "Leave the building, you fools!" he shouts. "It is *real*! It is *REAL*! Run for your lives!"

The sight of this pink-clad madman, a terrified audience member like themselves, threatening the front rows with what is obviously more than a magician's prop, causes the spectators within swinging distance to try to get away; even the musicians clamor out of the pit. Everyone stumbles toward the aisles. And when they get there, they keep on moving. Soon, the entire audience is panicking like a mob. There is pandemonium – women screaming, men shouting – and a rush for the exits.

Onstage, the giant lizard struggles to get free. It twists and turns, rattling the cage so violently it lifts off the floor . . . the beast's shoulders bulge through. It writhes again . . . and its midsection emerges . . . and then, with one last effort . . . it is out!

Bell has pulled the intended victim to the side and torn the gag from her mouth and the blindfold from her eyes. "I am Angelina Nottingham!" she is shouting. "I am Angelina Nottingham!" The lizard is moving straight ahead. It doesn't see her anymore. What it does see, directly in front of it . . . is Irene Doyle and Beatrice Leckie.

It makes for them.

Sherlock is too far away. It will kill one of them. He is frantic with fear. A strange thought rushes through his mind. Which girl would he save . . . if he could save just one? He also wonders what it was that Irene came to tell him at the apothecary shop yesterday. He pulls back his horsewhip and cracks it in the air, his fear giving him so much energy that the sound is like a gun going off, louder than any snap he has ever produced. It appears to frighten the lizard for an instant. It starts . . . and turns around, facing the source of the noise . . . Sherlock Holmes.

But it doesn't come at him. As it surveys the cage and the area around it on the stage, a homing instinct seems to seize it. It moves back toward its former prison, notices the winding stairs going down into the basement, and heads toward them.

Sherlock picks up the axe. He rushes after the beast. Its back is to him as they reach the top of the staircase.

"No!" cries Hemsworth. He runs toward the boy.

Holmes raises the axe above the dragon.

"No, Sherlock," says Beatrice under her breath.

But when the axe comes down, it doesn't rend the lizard in half. Instead, Holmes has aimed at the chain between the shackles holding the front and back feet together on the reptile's left side. *It will die if it tries to descend those stairs in shackles; it will fall to its death.* The blow breaks the chain.

But the lizard isn't in a thankful mood. It turns on Sherlock, its big, alligator-head fixed on him, flicking its forked tongue in his direction.

Irene rushes forward, distracting it. And as it turns to her, exposing its right side, Sherlock brings the axe down again, breaking the chain between the shackles there too. *It is completely free!* He shouts, and the dragon turns away from Irene and back to him once more. The boy raises the axe to its face. It turns and slithers away, down the staircase, just as Sherlock had hoped.

It moves at incredible speed. Holmes looks to the seats. Lestrade and his burly colleague are watching, aghast. Scuttle stands beside them, as stiff as a pillar, eyes ready to pop from his head and bounce onto the stage.

"Arrest those two!" Sherlock cries, motioning to the magicians. Nottingham is frozen behind the cage, in shock. Hemsworth, who had rushed across the stage to save his pet, is near Holmes, and both are close to the staircase – the one the lizard is descending. They both race after it.

With His Highness fleeing, Lestrade and his colleague concentrate their efforts on Nottingham, but he snaps from his numbed state and resists them. By the time they have him under control, Holmes, Hemsworth, and the dragon are gone.

It is just the three of them in the basement now. The big reptile reaches the bottom of the stairs and pounds across the floor on its enormous claws, its shackles clanking on the floor. When it gets to the staircase on the dressing-room side, it begins to climb. Sherlock, who is well ahead of Hemsworth, remembers that he left the little door open that leads to the passageway under the rooms. As he reaches the bottom of the staircase and looks up, he can barely make out the image of the dragon. But he can see where it goes: through the passage door . . . a perfect, tight fit.

Holmes isn't about to go in there with the creature. Instead, he climbs the stairs, his legs churning, his breathing heavy. He flings open the hallway entrance and runs toward Hemsworth's dressing room. He cannot recall if he closed the floorboards. It takes him mere seconds to arrive. He holds the door open a tiny crack to peer inside. Suddenly, the creature rams into him, knocking him back against the wall as it explodes through the doorway. *It smelled me at the door! It has incredible hunting instincts!* For an instance, the dragon is turned toward the far end of the hall. Hemsworth comes through the basement door. It spots him. *What should I do?* thinks Sherlock. *Why not let his pet kill him? But that wouldn't be right. It would be vengeance, not justice. I must be better than the villains.*

Sherlock shouts at the lizard to distract it. It looks at him, then turns back to Hemsworth. It, too, must make a choice. It chooses the boy.

Holmes is in an enclosed space. He has just one option. *Get outside!* He sprints down the hallway with the dragon in pursuit. He can't believe how fast it can move. At the door, Sherlock fumbles with the handle. The beast nears. Its huge tongue darts out at him. The boy turns the knob and rushes through. The skies have opened and it is pouring rain, making the evening prematurely dark. Sherlock can't take the time to close the door behind him. The dragon emerges into the soggy London night!

They are in the little courtyard behind the theater. The boy realizes he is leading the lizard. *It is following me! I must take it away from people.* He chooses the back alley that goes out to Jermyn Street. As he runs down it, boots smacking on the wet cobblestones, he hears Hemsworth pursuing them, shouting at the dragon as if it were a dog off its leash that must come home. *He IS mad!*

The boy is not just running for his life now, he is running for the lives of every Londoner in their path. He *must* choose a route that is nearly deserted. It helps that the night is inclement. But he knows that some citizens, poor folks mostly, are almost always on the streets. It is time to think like Malefactor again, use the alleys and mews and the narrowest little arteries.

He is well aware of why Malefactor came into his mind. It isn't just because of his rival's ability to navigate the back roads of London. *He is here.* Sherlock knows it. He could feel his presence when he got to the courtyard. The young crime lord and his minions are running, somewhere behind, waiting for their chance. He turns left off Jermyn Street, quickly finds an alley going south, and heads to where he tracked Miss Venus: toward the park at St. James Square. Surely not many pedestrians will be there in the rain. Sherlock hears a scream or two behind him, but it is so dark where he and the beast are going, mostly out of the gas-lit areas, and only under the lamps for brief stretches in pelting rain, that most of the people who *are* out don't even notice them. Sherlock keeps the dragon close to his heels, no more than twenty feet away and never out of sight. It seems to be fixed on him. He wonders if it really wants to kill him, or if it is terrified too, and just concentrating on a living thing it knows. From the square, he continues south-east, becoming drenched, but with an idea forming in his mind.

Within minutes he approaches Pall Mall Street, the elegant, wide avenue that runs from Trafalgar Square almost to Buckingham Palace. Private clubs are on the south side here, places where London's wealthy gentlemen go to drink, smoke cigars, read papers, and converse. Rich people don't go out into the rain; the place is deserted. Holmes sends the lizard past their wide front doors. Then Sherlock leads the creature to the far end of the queen's park. No one goes to a park in a downpour. He hopes the swans are farther to the west, closer to the palace. They would make quick, tasty meals. But there is no sign of them. The dragon slows on the grass here, so Sherlock slows too, tempting it to keep moving. They enter an alley on the far side of the park, rush down an artery past the Admiralty, and cross Whitehall Street, just a stone's throw from Scotland Yard.

But Sherlock isn't directing the murderous reptile to police headquarters. He doubts it would go willingly into a cell! He can smell the River Thames and knows he is nearing his goal.

Darting through the courtyard in Scotland Yard, breathing heavily, soaked to the skin, he screams as loudly as he can. Three constables come rushing out, one after the other. Though they miss seeing the boy pursued by the strange beast, they spot Hemsworth, still a suspect in the Nottingham case, running, looking raving mad in the dark London rain . . . apparently chasing someone. They pursue him. Sherlock enters a small street on the other side of the Yard, looks back to make sure the beast and everyone else is following, and somehow picks up his speed. They are on a downward slope and up ahead the boy can see a series of wharves and the dark surface of the river beyond that. There are few gaslights here. The rain begins to subside.

He leads the lizard right out onto a long wharf, well over the Thames. The water is deep here. His boots pound on the slippery, damp boards; the lizard's shackles clang. This seems the best place to corner the beast. First, it is far away from people. That is most important. Secondly, there are police officers to help. Thirdly, there are fishing nets on the wharves, some of them with thick-corded webs capable of holding a shark. They could be thrown over the big reptile to subdue it. If need be, the police (he is hoping at least one is armed with a revolver) can kill it, quickly and humanely, where no one will see it happen, or be injured in the action. He is praying they can capture it alive.

But the dragon does something he hadn't expected. Out at the end of the wharf sits a ship that is being refitted. Next to it is a raft about eight feet square, that workers must stand on while making repairs. When the creature nears Sherlock, almost at the edge, it spots the raft and slows to a crawl. Holmes, gasping for air, slips past his foe and gets to the land side of the wharf. The dragon comes to a halt at the very edge, looking down, examining the raft. It seems mesmerized.

Hemsworth, then the police, arrive on the wharf, some fifty feet away.

The magician moves closer. "It remembers," he says.

The officers of the Force, standing not far behind him, have no idea what that means, but it isn't a surprise that His Highness would say something incomprehensible – they believe he is loony. Neither can they make out what is happening way out there in the gloom at the far end of the wharf. All they know is that the boy whose voice they had heard screaming in their courtyard is still out there, even though his pursuer has stopped. "Is he committing suicide?" one of them asks.

Suddenly, the dragon drops off the end of the wharf and crashes onto the raft. The police rush forward. When they arrive, they are surprised to see the boy still standing there. They seize him as he looks down to the water. He is watching the creature on the floating boards below, as it grips the wood surface with it big claws, shackles still on its feet, artificial wings drooping on its back. It snaps at the rope that holds the raft to the boat, perhaps remembering the cords that held it to the cage. The rope tears free, and the little vessel begins to drift out into the muddy Thames in the diminishing rain. It has grown very dark, and none of the Bobbies notice the raft, but Sherlock watches the dragon looking back at its tormentors, as if satisfied to be free of them, and London, and human civilization. Within seconds, it is just an outline on its boat in the water, nearly beyond sight, going east and picking up speed, toward the North Sea and the ocean.

"Is there something out there?" asks one officer, squinting into the night.

Downriver, on the next wharf, Sherlock sees the silhouettes of three figures watching the dragon drift by. One wears a black tailcoat.

Hemsworth stares across the rainy river toward the sea. "It remembers," he repeats.

FINAL ACT

I t takes Sherlock Holmes a few minutes to convince the constables to bring Hemsworth back to the Scotland Yard offices. Nothing has been proven against him in the Nottingham case, they insist (two of them had seen the amazing hat feat with their own eyes), and it isn't a crime to chase someone in the night. So, the boy has to tell a lie, explaining that His Highness was trying to force him off the wharf and into the water. Hemsworth smirks at this, but then Holmes also assures them that once they get to the Yard, Lestrade's son will be there with more serious allegations against the magician.

His Highness goes without resisting, though he glances back at the water a few times as they usher him away.

There is a rain-soaked crowd entering the offices as they reach the door.

Lestrade Jr. and his colleague have a sour Nottingham by the arms, and trailing is a motley crew of theatergoers: Sigerson Bell, Irene Doyle, Beatrice Leckie, Angelina Nottingham, and even little Scuttle, who lags a good distance behind. When Sherlock sees Irene, he remembers again that she has some-thing she wants to tell him.

But before he enters, Bell takes him aside. "My boy, I cannot go in there. My, shall we say, unorthodox appearance, may not be helpful in presenting the case against these gentlemen."

"You saw it."

"Yes, I did."

"It was real."

"Yes, it was. This world is not yet all unveiled, my boy; never will be, even when it is all physically discovered. There may still be dinosaurs among us."

"And there is more in this world than is dreamt of in any human being's imagination."

"Indeed, there is."

The Senior Inspector, working late as usual, happens to be striding out to the reception room as the crowd enters. He almost falls on the floor when he sees Nottingham, then gapes at Hemsworth, and looks very concerned, indeed, when he spots Sherlock Holmes. Scuttle slumps in late, almost unnoticed.

The outside door hasn't yet closed, and through it Lestrade sees Hobbs from *The Times of London* approaching as quickly as his little feet can propel his rotund body. Behind him are two journalists he recognizes: Hilton Poke from *The News of the World* and Simpson Small from *The Illustrated Police News*. Behind them . . . is a swarm of their colleagues.

"Secure the doors!" the Inspector shouts. The thick wooden entrances are slammed shut and barred.

"Someone speak!" exclaims Lestrade, "and dear God, let it not be Sherlock Holmes."

His son clears his throat. "Sir . . . it . . . it was all a trick."

"An illusion," corrects Nottingham, pronouncing the word with syrupy elegance.

"An illusion, yes," continues the young detective.

"I was informed that Hemsworth had a . . ." begins Nottingham.

"A discovery," says His Highness.

Nottingham smiles back, "yes, a discovery. And it occurred to me that I could use said discovery to create my greatest illusion."

"*Our* greatest illusion."

"Yes, of course, *ours*. I had found a marvelous place beneath The World's End Hotel, when I purchased that establishment under the name of Riyah. I wanted to keep it secret and rarely went there during the day. Thus, when His Highness approached me, I had a perfect holding place for this . . . discovery. So, using my genius and . . . his discovery . . . we made a dragon appear on the London stage, and then we used you," he glances at everyone in sight, "and put you all into a little play that began with the supposed murder of yours truly, a furious pursuit by the boy wonder Sherlock Holmes – a source on the streets told us about him – and the aging and unspectacular Inspector Lestrade. We needed the boy, since we felt the police alone would not be able to follow our clues sufficiently to make the game work. He, also, we were told, is willing to break the rules, while the Force is, shall we say, conservative."

Lestrade steps forward and seizes both Hemsworth and

Nottingham by the collars simultaneously. They are both big men but he slams them down onto a bench.

"I will thank you to keep your hands off me," snaps Nottingham, "you boor!"

"You have no charges against us!" adds Hemsworth.

"Other than being ugly . . . do we have any?" asks Lestrade, turning to his son.

"Forcible confinement and kidnapping," says Sherlock Holmes.

"I have a solicitor of the highest standing," responds the Wizard, "we shall be out within a few years, perhaps months."

"And attempted murder!" cries young Lestrade.

"Of whom?" asks his father.

Sherlock considers suggesting Scuttle, to begin with, but realizes that Hemsworth and Nottingham will simply say that they had caught the lad trespassing and had no plans to kill him. The beast has vanished. *Best stick to his wife.*

"Of her!" Young Lestrade points at Mrs. Nottingham. In all the confusion, his father hasn't noticed the woman in stage makeup wrapped in a police coat. He turns to her with surprise. "I thought you were in Europe."

Angelina simply shakes her head.

"She was the woman in the cage with the dragon, Father."

"She? I thought that was Miss Venus."

"Of course, you did," murmurs Nottingham.

"We murdered no one. And our solicitor shall prove it!" shrieks Hemsworth, getting to his feet and advancing on his former wife so aggressively that a constable decides to step between them. "And he will also prove that this *prostitute*, who went by the name of my wife and Nottingham's, is a philandering excuse for a woman . . . who deserved what she got."

"And whom you treated like dirt long before she did anything wrong!" says Irene Doyle, "Whom you and your empty-headed, fame-seeking cohort here intended to murder in front of a London crowd, in the most gruesome fashion. Sit down, sir!"

Hemsworth actually sits.

"So," muses Inspector Lestrade, looking amazed, "they were going to . . ."

"The dragon was going to kill her tonight, Father . . . and devour her . . . in front of the crowd."

Mrs. Nottingham buries her head.

"Yes, well then, there indeed is that small point of *attempted* murder," says Lestrade. Then he looks with concern at his son. "Did you say the *dragon*, young man?"

"You will have to prove that," remarks Hemsworth, before young Lestrade can answer.

"Do you deny that you harbored a vicious beast . . . a giant lizard that you found somewhere past the far reaches the civilized world?" says Sherlock.

"You, Master Holmes, are a fantasist, as I told you once before."

"Do you deny it?"

"I do."

"*A giant lizard*, Master Holmes, is that what I heard you say?" asks Lestrade. "Perhaps I should let in the press, after all. They shall be glad to quote you saying such a thing and place it in their papers for all to read . . . as will I."

"Let them in, if you must, Inspector, and we shall discuss your errors in this case."

"And where is your dragon now, Master Holmes?" demands Lestrade angrily.

"It got away."

"Away? How convenient! Do you expect me, and the London populace, to really believe that these two circus clowns had a real, living and fire-breathing dragon harbored in our city, and that they were going to use it to murder this woman?"

"Not fire-breathing, sir, and not, technically, a dragon."

"Then what?"

"A creature Hemsworth found somewhere, a creature unknown to the Western World at this time."

"I can vouch for the existence of the dragon, sir," says Lestrade Jr., a little shakily.

His father is taken aback by his son's courage. "Oh?"

"Many people saw it tonight at the theater."

"Many people saw it many times," smirks Hemsworth, "over the last few months. But no one in their right mind believes it was anything other than a magical creation . . . a discovery."

Nottingham laughs with him.

"But you did intend to kill her . . . with whatever you had on that stage?" barks Lestrade.

"I should like to see anyone prove that!" snaps Hemsworth.

"Out with it! What was it? What fiendish creation did you have?"

"That sir," says Nottingham, "is our little secret. Magician's privileges: artists' rights."

"YOU SIR!" cries Scuttle suddenly leaping to his feet and working his way into view, "is no artiste!" Nottingham and Hemsworth, who hadn't noticed the little boy until this very moment, are shocked to see him alive, though the Wizard then looks over at Sherlock and nods his head in admiration. Master Scuttle turns to the whole group. "I . . . I has a confessionment to make. I says I knows wagonload-ings of famous celebritants . . . but I don't. I never gabbed with the queen, not once, nor Florence Nightingale nor the Spring 'eeled Jack. But I thought it was important to remark that I did. But I don't think so now. They was going to feed me to their beast! They did it for their public publicity, for their money, and their famousness. And that, though many thinks is important, is not. I don't likes famous people anymore. Not at all. I never actually spoke to one in my 'ole life . . . and I don't care if I ever do!"

He runs to the door, unlocks it and races out.

"Peasant," sneers Nottingham.

"You, Inspector," says Hemsworth, ignoring Scuttle's exit completely, "may charge us with attempted murder, if you believe we harbored a mythical beast, and can prove it. I am willing to tell the press, this very night, that you are in search of . . . a dragon. Otherwise, charge us with the lesser crime of confinement, and we shall take our medi-cine, light as I suspect that will be. If you cannot make the creature appear before the magistrates . . . you have no murder weapon."

Lestrade pauses. "We . . . uh . . . are not in the business of dragon hunting. There need not be any word of that. But we shall certainly convict you both of holding this woman against her will. And it shall ruin your careers!"

"I think not," retorts Hemsworth. "Any publicity is good publicity. Our trick is still in the midst of its performance, as it were, still paying dividends. I will wager you whatever you like, that we will come from prison bigger theater stars than we are now; that we shall step upon the London stage when we return . . . as legends."

"And I will wager *you*, sir, whatever you like," says Sherlock Holmes, "that you are a despicable human being, and so is your villainous partner. And if no one else on earth knows it, I do, and God does in heaven, and somewhere deep in your dark hearts, you do too, and that . . . is enough."

Lestrade soon clears the room, instructing his charges to take both men into custody, that Mrs. Nottingham be tended to at Bartholomew Hospital, and everyone not in the employ of the Force remove themselves from the premises.

But as Sherlock tries to leave the room, Hemsworth takes him by the arm and brings his lips up close to the boy's ear.

"I found it in the Indian Ocean. It was the most remarkable thing. It was floating on a raft, debris, I think, from some cursed boat that had gone down way out there. It must have walked onto that wood as it neared wherever it lived, perhaps some godforsaken island at the edge of the world. Perhaps it fell asleep there, and then, it was carried out to sea. I thought I was dreaming. . . . There must be more of them in the wilderness, somewhere!"

Sherlock pushes him away and goes through the door at a brisk pace. The men from the press, who are still not allowed in, ignore him at first, but then both Hobbs and Poke recognize him.

"Master Holmes, do you have a comment? Do you know anything about this?"

Sherlock pauses. This is his chance. He can at least take credit for what he has accomplished.

"No," he says.

Sigerson Bell catches up to him just as he speaks.

"That's my boy."

They trudge toward White Hall Street.

"Really," Holmes finally says, "I achieved nothing. We were played for fools."

"Nonsense, you saved a woman's life, and a precious boy's, too."

Sherlock doesn't respond.

"But you also did something much more important than that."

"And what was that, sir?" demands his apprentice, stopping suddenly. "They won't serve much time in prison. They may even gain in the long run."

"But the key in life, my boy, is not to be like the saint

in the Golden Legend, who slew the dragon, saving the princess and her country, gaining fame and fortune as his prize. It isn't the key at all. Rewards often come to people who don't deserve them: they are often misplaced in our world. You must turn *yourself* into gold. Here is what matters about what transpired over the past few weeks, Sherlock Holmes, here is what is more important than anything else . . . you, my young knight, did what was right."

The yellow fog is heavy now, and Bell seems to disappear into it as he speaks. He is magically replaced by Irene Doyle, who has caught up from behind.

"I had something I wanted to tell you, at the apothecary shop yesterday." Her voice is shaky and it scares him.

"Yes?"

"I . . . I am going away . . . to America, for a long time."

"Away?"

"It's an opportunity, a good one . . . for training in the opera. It will be respectable . . . Father says I should . . . so I cannot . . ." her voice trails off. She kisses him tenderly on the cheek and disappears, too.

He is all alone now. Instead of going directly to the shop, he wants the air and takes a longer route, this time through the West End, the theater district, trying to convince himself that it is good Irene is gone . . . that she may come back. He walks by the Adelphi Theatre, the magnificent Lyceum, and finally the Royal Opera House. He used to visit it with his mother as a boy, not inside with the people who mattered, but listening at a coal grate at the back.

He sees the famous names on the marquees, hears the few remaining pedestrians talking about this great man or that beautiful lady, what they did upon the stage tonight, who they know, who they are sweet on. It all sounds so very important to them. *Their minds are filled with illusions.* On the streets, he meets poor children in bare feet, begging. They remind him of Scuttle.

In this time of spectacle in the empire, thinks Sherlock, it is difficult to *really* know what is right and what is wrong, what to value. He wants to quit, not worry about such things, spend time with his dying father, live a normal life. The shadow that is following him up Bow Street at this very moment would vanish then. He could go to Beatrice in Southwark, right now.

But something stops him. *You saved a woman's life and a precious boy's, too.* "I am almost there," he says out loud. He fixes his necktie, and straightens his waistcoat and frock coat. "If a sword of justice is needed," he says, even louder, not caring who hears, ". . . then I shall be it!"

Vanishing Girl is a story in which Holmes is powerfully developed. The reader discovers the origins of his learning self-defense and his infatuation with scientific "potions" . . . to help solve crimes. Highly Recommended." – *CM Magazine*

Foreword Magazine's Book of the Year, Gold

Arthur Ellis Award / Best Juvenile Book

IODE Violet Downey Book Award

**Moonbeam Awards Intermediate
Middle Grades Category, Gold**

Geoffrey Bilson Award for Historical Fiction

Silver Birch Honour Book

CLA's Book of the Year for Children Honour Book

Booklist Top Ten in Youth Mysteries

**Ontario Library Association's Top Ten
Young Adult Fiction Books of the Year List**

**Best Books for Kids and Teens List
(Canadian Children's Book Centre)**

Books of Note List (Tristate YA Review Committee)

EYE OF THE CROW

It is the spring of 1867, and a yellow fog hangs over London. In the dead of night, a woman is brutally stabbed and left to die in a pool of blood. No one sees the terrible crime. Or so it seems.

Nearby, a brilliant, bitter boy dreams of a better life. He is the son of a Jewish intellectual and a highborn lady – social outcasts – impoverishment the price of their mixed marriage. The boy's name is Sherlock Holmes.

Strangely compelled to visit the scene, Sherlock comes face to face with the young Arab wrongly accused of the crime. By degrees, he is drawn to the center of the mystery, until he, too, is a suspect.

Danger runs high in this desperate quest for justice. As the clues mount, Sherlock sees the murder through the eye of its only witness. But a fatal mistake and its shocking consequence change everything and put him squarely on a path to becoming a complex man with a dark past – and the world's greatest detective.

DEATH IN THE AIR

Still reeling from his mother's death, brought about by his involvement in solving London's brutal East End murder, young Sherlock Holmes commits himself to fighting crime . . . and is soon immersed in another case.

While visiting his father at work, Sherlock stops to watch a dangerous high-trapeze performance, framed by the magnificent glass ceiling of the legendary Crystal Palace. But without warning, the aerialist drops, screaming and flailing to the floor. He lands with a sickening thud, just feet away and rolls almost onto the boy's boots. He is bleeding profusely and his body is grotesquely twisted. Leaning over, Sherlock brings his ear up close. "Silence me . . ." the man gasps and then lies still. In the mayhem that follows, the boy notices something amiss that no one else sees – and he knows that foul play is afoot. What he doesn't know is that his discovery will set him on a trail that leads to an entire gang of notorious and utterly ruthless criminals.

VANISHING GIRL

When a wealthy young socialite mysteriously vanishes in Hyde Park, young Sherlock Holmes is compelled to prove himself once more. There is much at stake: the kidnap victim, an innocent child's survival, the fragile relationship between himself and the beautiful Irene Doyle. Sherlock must act quickly if he is to avoid the growing menace of his enemy, Malefactor, and further humiliation at the hands of Scotland Yard.

As twisted and dangerous as the backstreets of Victorian London, this third case in The Boy Sherlock Holmes series takes the youth on a heart-stopping race against time to the countryside, the coast, and into the haunted lair of exotic – and deadly – night creatures.

Despite the cold, the loneliness, the danger, and the memories of his shattered family, one thought keeps Sherlock going; soon, very soon, the world will come to know him as the master detective of all time.

THE SECRET FIEND

I n 1868, Benjamin Disraeli becomes England's first
Jewish-born prime minister. Sherlock Holmes wel-
comes the event – but others fear it. The upper classes
worry that the black-haired Hebrew cannot be good
for the empire. The wealthy hear rumblings as the poor
hunger for sweeping improvements to their lot in life. The
winds of change are blowing.

Late one night, Sherlock's admirer and former school-
mate, Beatrice, arrives at his door, terrified. She claims a
maniacal, bat-like man has leapt upon her and her friend on
Westminster Bridge. The fiend she describes is the Spring
Heeled Jack, a fictional character from the old Penny
Dreadful thrillers. Moreover, Beatrice declares the Jack has
made off with her friend. She begs Holmes to help, but he
finds the story incredible. Reluctant to return to detective
work, he pays little heed – until the attacks increase, and
Spring Heeled Jacks seem to be everywhere. Now, all of
London has more to worry about than politics. Before he
knows it, the unwilling boy detective is thrust, once more,
into the heart of a deadly mystery, in which everyone, even
his closest friend and mentor, is suspect.